Super Market Love Affair & Three Short Stories

I0591572

Introduction:

This book is a combination of several stories that encompass the full spectrum of human emotions. As you read you will find loneness, addiction, abuse, adventure, and of course love. It is all fantasy of course, but it is taken from our being human. I hope you enjoy and possibly get a laugh or two from the following pages.

Supermarket Love Affair

ISBN: 978-0-578-55712-0

Three Short Stories

ISBN: 978-0-578-56641-2

Combined ISBN: EPUB

978-0-578-59048-6

Copyright: 2019

Supermarket Love Affair

CHAPTERS

Supermarket Love Affair

ONE

One beautiful late spring day as I decided to pick up a few items before heading home and spending the evening by myself and with my furry companions, decided to stop and spend a few minutes shopping at my local Roscoe's supermarket. I had a funny feeling; you know when your fifth sense kicks in as I shopped that someone was watching me. I thought that I was being covertly observed from a short distance by a very attractive woman about my age. Let me first introduce myself, my name is Calvino Hobart, age fifty, widowed, unattached and owner of Royal Charter Transportation and Hobart trucking company. I was dressed in my usual attire, blue jeans, loafers, t-shirt and a sports jacket. I shop at my local Roscoe's as needed; maybe once or twice a week. I like being out of the house and is one of the reasons, besides catching sales why I shop a couple times a week. This particular time I noticed a well-dressed and very attractive woman with stockings and high heels, skirt just above the knee, blouse and a matching jacket to the skirt, nice figure, and smooth flawless skin with a slight olive complexion. Her makeup wasn't heavy and her brunet hair was long but in a twist in back. She appeared to be around my age or maybe younger, and I really admired her very feminine appearance, something you don't see often now since women wear pant suits, jeans and tights now more than when I was younger. I had a shopping cart and had decided to try to shop for the week since I had some extended business that would be occupying more of my time and needed to purchase a little more than I usually do, but that didn't seem to be working for me at all this day.

After entering the store and retrieving a shopping cart, stopped at and used a couple of the sanitary wipes from the kiosk by the front door and wiped the cart handle off before starting my shopping adventure. I pulled my short shopping list from my jacket pocket before entering the produce section. I first chose several items, grapes and oranges, then some fresh vegetables and placed them in the plastic produce bags that are available. I had jalapeno and bell peppers, celery, and several other vegetables, before I grabbed a bag of onions and a three pound bag of red potatoes. After leaving the produce section, and then entering the bakery section, that's when I first really noticed the well-dressed woman nearby. I couldn't help but notice her because most people don't dress for a trip to the supermarket. And as I looked at her, and admired her, I figured maybe she had gotten off work and was just stopping to buy a few things before going home. For some reason she intrigued me, she was very beautiful and it had been a while since I had paid much attention to any one woman in particular.

I continued on my weekly shopping adventure and after glancing at some of the sale items in the low coolers and checking the buy one, get one free section, before I proceeded to ply the isles. I didn't get any perishable items that needed immediate refrigeration; I stopped basically because I needed vegetables, cat food and a bag of litter. But I liked walking the isles and noticing new items and picking up some real bargain items when I happened upon them.

I headed to the first isle that contained many boxed items. That's when it seemed to me that I was being followed. She, this beautiful well-dressed woman walked past me and stopped down the aisle in front of me a short distance. As I approached she stopped me, and asked if I would hand her an item from the top shelf. I asked her which one, she responded in a very pleasant soft voice as she pointed to the item she wanted. I reached and handed her the item and she thanked me. Told her, you're welcome, and complimented her on her appearance before I then continued down the aisle. I continued to the end and around to the next aisle and came upon some items on my list and shortly after the attractive woman came around to the same aisle. She stopped just short of where I was standing and said excuse me, but could I help her again. I said sure, what does the young lady desire. She asked again if I could hand her another item from on the very top shelf. I handed her the item she requested. It seemed to me she could have reached the item she wanted as I handed it to her. I said maybe we should just shop together and introduced myself to her and complimented her on her very lovely appearance. She said her name was Renee Simone, and she stated that maybe we should. I told her it would be a pleasure to shop with such a beautiful woman as you. We did and about half an hour later we were standing at the checkout after having a very pleasant conversation as we shopped. She checked out ahead of me and after having done so, stood waiting for me. After paying for my items, I asked her if I could help her load her bags into her automobile. She only had two bags and said she had decided to walk to the store and lived in a nearby condo building. I offered her a ride home, and she accepted and I loaded her groceries into the back seat of my auto and placed mine in the trunk. I opened the door for her and she gracefully got inside as I took and returned the shopping cart to the cart corral.

When I entered my auto, I asked if she had anything that was perishable. She responded no that she had only purchased a few dry items. I asked if she would grace my presence and accept an invitation to dinner with me now. I explained I was a widower and hadn't been to dinner with anyone since my wife passed away and would enjoy dinning with her. Renee said it would be her pleasure and that she was also a widower. I asked her if she had any preferences as to what or where she would like to eat. She said it was completely up to me, and was just thrilled that I had invited her and thanked me for being so considerate. I drove to the Reds Sea Food World restaurant which wasn't very far away and were known for their excellent dishes, and we weren't that far away from Roscoe's as I pulled into their lot and parked. I came around and opened the door for Mrs. Simone, and admired her beautiful and shapely legs. We entered and I asked for a booth for two. And were shown and seated in a small comfortable and very intimate booth. I told Mrs. Simone it was completely on me and to order anything she wanted because it was a pleasure being in the company of one as beautiful as she. A smile came to her face, as she stated that she had dressed up to go shopping after being alone for fourteen months and just wanted to feel good about herself and hadn't worn some of her clothes for such long time and hoped they still fitted her. Said she hoped that I didn't feel like she was stalking me, but said she found me attractive, and her first impression was I looked like I might be a nice person. I thanked her for the compliment and said it has been almost eighteen months since my wife departed and how different it was to be alone, after having had the pleasure of someone close for so long, and I hadn't been out to dinner with anyone until now. She stated that was so true, especially if you really loved someone. The waitress came to our table and handed us the menus. I asked Mrs. Simon if she cared for a glass of wine, she responded that would be wonderful, and I ordered two glasses of Pinot Noir. The waitress departed and when she returned with the wine we were ready to order after looking over the menus. Mrs. Simone ordered the bountiful platter, with a baked potato and coleslaw, and I ordered the seafood festival platter, with brown rice and coleslaw. Mrs. Simone stated that she had only been out to dinner with some distant relatives when they came to visit, and hadn't really been out since her husband had passed away. Said she wanted to thank me for asking her out to dinner, and that it made her feel good that someone had found her attractive. Said she was fifty two and hadn't thought of being older until lately, and believed much of those thoughts came from being alone.

Asked me what line of work was I involved with? Stated that I was in the transportation industry and operated a trucking company and charter tour bus company. I was also involved in some real-estate operations. I said to her before she even asked that my wife was fifty five years old and had died of a massive stroke, and that I was just coming to terms with her death. I also told her it was hard and never expected the grieving process to take so long, and just applied myself to my work as a way to keep my mind off of her not being here, but that was even difficult since she had worked in the business with me. She responded that it had been very difficult for her also, and that she had found a part time job at the nearby discount store to fill her abundance of time, and also knitted to stay busy. Said her husband had worked for the railroad and was killed in a derailment, along with several other people. She was thankful that he had left her with ample insurance, but the money didn't compensate for all the loneliness.

Our food arrived and the pace of the conversation slowed as we ate. Said to her I was hungry and had planned on cooking when I arrived at home, until I met you, and was very happy you took me up on my offer because one of the most difficult things has been eating alone. She agreed with my assessment, and was very thankful that I had asked her out. When we finished eating and the waitress came back and asked if we wanted any dessert, we both declined. She returned shortly and placed the bill on the table; I paid and left a tip.

As we departed I asked Mrs. Simone for her address, and shortly after leaving the restaurant pulled up in front of her building. I got out and helped her out and retrieved her bags from the back seat and walked with her to the front entrance door. She asked me inside. I declined and said I needed to go home and feed my cats. I told her how much I truly enjoyed her company and again told her how very beautiful she was. I handed her my business card, but I wrote my cell number on the back. I told her it had been a real pleasure, and stated that I would like to see you again if it was all right with her, and would wait until she was safely inside before I departed. She soon waved to me from her second floor balcony a few minutes after entering her unit, and I drove home. I didn't ask her for her number because I would leave it up to her if we went out again.

When I arrived home, pulled up my driveway and parked inside my garage. I removed my bags from the trunk of the car, closed the garage door and walked across the back yard looking at the grass before unlocking the back door. Entered and was greeted by my two feline friends Pits and Patter. They rubbed up against my leg as I headed to the kitchen and they followed. I placed the grocery bags on the counter and bent down and petted them both. I removed their empty bowls from the feeding stand and made some dish water and washed their bowls, setting them in the dish rack to drain and picked up their water bowl and washed it also. I opened two cans of cat food and placed each in their respective bowls. Mixed it up and placed them back in the stand as they both eagerly started eating before I returned the fresh water dish to the stand. I checked their litter box and cleaned it. After washing my hands I began putting the few groceries I had purchased away.

I walked around the house and found everything in order, before heading to the bedroom to undress. Then taking a nice long hot shower and putting on some clean shorts and a t-shirt before returning to the kitchen to grab a cold can of beer from the fridge and pouring it in a glass. I went to my home office and placed my cell phone on charge. Since I had gone to dinner it was a little later than usual, before going to the living room and turning on the television to the evening news. I sat back and thought how nice it was to have eaten with someone, and how beautiful she appeared to be. I didn't ask for her number because if she wanted to see me again, I would rather it be when she was ready.

The evening out with Mrs. Simone, really put something on my mind since it had been such a seemingly long time since I had socialized with anyone other than my employees and a few family members. Sue's family and I weren't close other than the occasional phone call or Christmas card, and what remained of my family amounted to about the same. Basically I was a lonely, middle aged, widowed bachelor. I must say that I did enjoy dinner with Mrs. Simone very much and now realize just how lonely I really was, especially since I was in the mist of being bought out of my transport business, and figured it was time for a real change of pace. There was a larger interstate trucking operation and they were consolidating several midsized and small operators like me in order to expand nationwide and the companies like mine were the one with fleets of tractors and a base of operations. I operated in several states and locally. They had placed and offer on the table of $65,000,000.00 dollars for my fleet operations of ninety five trucks and trailers, and that also included my terminal, and assume all the debt associated with my company. I also had another offer for my charter bus operation that was from a separate company. I had fifty-one busses, and there offer was for $30,000,000.00 dollars, to include the garage which was state of the art and very modern and up to date, and allowed me to operate and maximize my maintenance cost. I decided it would be best if I sold both and invested elsewhere and in more real estate. The business was constantly changing and I really needed a change and had my broker's license and only used it for my own investments. After Sue passed away I had put my all my energy into my operations, but now I felt I needed a real change. The two offers weren't connected but how often would they both come at the same time, and being ready for a real change in my life also, had decided to sell. My two furry friends came and joined me on the couch. Pits, my Russian blue came and rubbed against my leg before climbing next to me as I petted him and then Patter, my all black tabby jumped in my lap and she began kissing my hand, wanting to be petted. It had been just Pits and Patter, since Sue passed away. I decided to go to bed early, turned everything off and headed to the bedroom after checking the windows and doors. I pulled the covers back and climbed in and soon was joined by Patter as she climbed next to me and Pits climbed and sleep at my head. I could hear them purring as I fell asleep.

TWO

I woke up early, around six and Pits was at the foot of the bed and Patter was licking my ear. My two friends were always there for me, as I sat up, picking them both up and petting them. It was time for me to start another day. It was Thursday and would call my attorney later and inform him of my decision to sell both of my transportation assets. It was time to start a new life, a new career, maybe even a new house. I dragged my ass out of bed and relieved myself, and taking a shower before starting my day. I checked Pits and Patters bowls and cleaned them and fed them first before fixing myself breakfast. After eating I cleaned up and dressed in my usual attire, t-shirt, jeans, socks and running shoes and my sports coat. I checked that the toilet was clean and the lid up. Pits and Patter drank out the toilet sometimes, I guess because the water was cool. I petted them before I left as they sat on their cat tower sunning themselves and looking out the window as I went to the garage, getting in my car and backing out, then closing the garage door as I headed to work.

I stopped at the local gas station and filled my tank and purchased a newspaper and lotto ticket before heading to my office which was in a moderate size but very modern office building located between my trucking operation and charter bus service which was a separate piece of property. It was small compared to other office buildings but very efficient, there were several large offices on the first floor, and all were rented out. And I was located on the second floor with a view of both my operations from a large bay window since my office was located in the center of the building over the entrance and could observe them whenever I wanted. It was nine o'clock when I called my attorney and informed him of my decision to sell. He said he would contact the buyers and he would be in touch. I had built both of my businesses from the ground up over twenty-five years, and didn't feel inspired any longer especially after Sue departed. The business reminded me so much of her. She worked with me from day one, was my dispatcher and then my secretary and best friend. I didn't really know what I was going to do but wanted more free time to myself and a real change of pace. Just before lunch my attorney called me back and said that both buyers had accepted my selling price which was $500,000.00 more than their initial offers and were prepared to close possibly next week. I said great, they would keep all the employees which was one of my greatest concerns. He said they only had to make arrangements with the bank and the deals would be done. I thanked him and said he would be in contact with me once he had the dates and location, stated all the papers needed were already drawn up since they were both deals were waiting for me to make a decision. That the buyers of the trucking company were sending in a couple of people to see the operations and would be calling on me very soon. He said that was all for now and hung up.

I checked my phone and there were several missed calls, only one had left a voice mail as I proceeded to check it. When I did it was from Mrs. Simone, she asked that I call her back sometime today, and this was her number where she could be reached at any time. I saved it into my contacts and added her name. I phoned her after saving her number and she answered after the third ring. Said who I was and she was happy I had returned her call so soon. She asked if I would take her to the movies, it would be her treat if I did. I asked when she wanted to go. She said this evening or tomorrow or whatever was convenient for me. I said this afternoon would be fine. We decided on six pm and I would pick her up at her condo. I hung up and checked with my secretary if there was anything that needed my attention and told her I had decided to leave early. It was noon and headed home as I thought about Mrs. Simone. She was a mature woman and very pretty and besides what we talked about yesterday had given me the impression she was a home body and down to earth, even though I actually knew very little about her. Well when you meet someone it's not like they have their autobiography hanging around there neck. I needed to start having fun again and being with people other than on the job. I arrived home and Patter greeted me and I picked her up and petted her, then set her down on her cat tower, took out there comb, and combed her out and soon we were joined by Pits and I did the same for him and soon they were happy and continued with cleaning themselves. I undressed and laid down and took a short nap after setting my alarm clock to wake me at four pm.

I woke before the alarm went off, and showered, came out and decided to wear a summer suit with a light weight knit shirt, oiled my body and used some cologne, brushed my hair and shaved, then made sure Pits and Patter had food and water and a clean box. I called Mrs. Renee Simone; it was a quarter to five and said I was on my way. I arrived and parked in front of her building and walked up to the entrance and entered and found her door bell, pressed and waited, a voice said yes, and I said it was Calvino Hobart. I was bussed in, walked to the second floor and a door opened and there stood Mrs. Renee Simone. She was dressed in a smart brown outfit, skirt with a thin sheer summer blouse, matching light weight jacket, sheer brown stockings with brown open toe hi-heels, earrings and matching necklace and bracelet, her makeup was light and her skin was flawless. I complimented her on her appearance. She was ready and reached for a brown purse that matched her shoes and took out a set of keys and closed the door behind her, before locking it and we went downstairs and exited the building. I opened the car door for her and she stepped in. The theater wasn't very far and when we arrived, I parked and we walked to the entrance, she had a graceful walk and a really beautiful figure. We entered; she stated that this was the first time in more than two years of having been out past seven in the evening and about the same when it came to going out. I purchased tickets for a sci-fi thriller that she wanted to see. She was very pleasant to be with and I was surprised when she grabbed and held my hand during a tense moment in the movie.

When it was over, I asked if she was hungry. She wasn't starving but a light meal would do. I asked if she had any suggestions, and said a pizza would be perfect. I drove to a famous pizza restaurant and we went inside and were seated in a booth and given menus. I ordered two large glasses of red wine and we decided on a thin crust deluxe 16 inch pizza. The waiter took our order and returned with our wine. As we sat and talked, Renee said she thought that I was a pleasant person to be with again and would like to go out more often if it was ok with me. I said sure and that I enjoyed her company very much.

She said that she sensed that there was something on my mind. I told her that I was selling both of my companies and was undecided as to what I might do after I had divested myself of them. That I was going on a new life adventure and had no idea what or where it would take me. Was even thinking of selling my house and moving elsewhere, maybe to the next county west of here where there was more open space. She said that sounded wonderful. She had given some thought also of maybe moving elsewhere, but was skeptical because of her age and her surroundings were familiar and was scared that being alone would make her more susceptible to being victimized. I told her sometimes you just have to take a chance and follow your mind.

Our food arrived and we served ourselves. She said that I had made her feel much better about herself and that she had only been out with girlfriends and it wasn't the same as having someone like a man by your side, and that she wanted to be honest and upfront with me.

Asked if I would stay with her tonight, she didn't know what might happen but just wanted to be held, that I appeared to be someone that was trust worthy and she was willing to take a chance. She asked if I was shocked by what she had just asked of me. I said no, not really and it would be my pleasure to hold you and talk, and get to know you better, and said I was overjoyed she had asked me, because I didn't want to seem aggressive, but really welcomed her company.

We ate the pizza and it was very good. When we finished, I paid the bill and we went out and as I held the car door for her I took her hand and kissed it. She got in the car, and after I had gotten in, she turned to me and thanked me for taking her out, that she was feeling much better about herself, and asked if I would stop and get a bottle of wine on our way to her apartment. I said she only had to ask, and stopped at the Liquor World Store; they carry a very good selection of products and have a wonderful selection. I asked if she would come inside with me and help with the selection. Yes she replied, and asked if she had any preferences. She said a Pinot Noir or Petite Shiraz would be fine as we found several and decided on a couple of mid-priced ones. I made the purchase and we returned to the automobile, and held the door for her. She thanked me and got in. I drove to her condo and she directed me to park in the guest parking area in back, and pulled from her purse a placard and handed it to me and asked me to hang it from the rear view mirror which I did. I stepped out and around and opened the door for her, removed the bag containing the wine and we walked to the rear entrance of her building.

We entered and walked upstairs to her unit, she opened the door and I entered into a beautifully decorated apartment, it was clean and fresh. I removed my shoes and told her I don't wear shoes inside my home. She said that was great because she didn't ether. She directed me to the kitchen, and I sat the wine on the counter top. I asked if I could wash my hands and she showed me to one of two bathrooms. Her apartment was spacious, two bedrooms and baths, living and dining room and kitchen, there was also a balcony. When I returned from washing my hands found Renee in the kitchen, she had the wine opener and two glasses, and asked me if I would do the honors of opening one of the wines, and would place the other in the fridge. I opened one and she picked up the glasses and we went to the living room and sat on the couch. She had removed her jacket and I could see she wore no bra and had nice firm breast and her nipples were perky through the thin cotton material. I took my jacket off and laid it on a matching chair.

She had turned the radio on and before we sat down she grabbed my hand. I turned and faced her, as she asked me to hold her. I held her and felt her warm body as she pressed her breast against my chest. I rubbed her back, as she looked me in the eyes and said it felt so good to be held again as she wrapped her arms around me. After a minute I loosened my hold on her as she slowly released me. We then sat on the couch, and she sat right next to me. I poured the wine into the glasses, handed her one and I proposed a toast, to a lasting friendship, we clicked glasses and sipped the warm wine. She asked if I would like some ice, yes I replied as she rose and went to the kitchen and returned shortly with a bowl with some ice cubes, and placed several cubes each in our glasses.

She turned to me and said what she really wanted was for me to make love to her, that it was crazy and probably stupid, but she was dying to have sex with a real man, and the past year without was beginning to become unnerving and had hoped yesterday when we met that I had come inside with her. But when I said I had to go but gave her my business card, it let her know that I wasn't out to take advantage of her. I said to her it would be more than wonderful to hold her as I reached and pulled her close and kissed her. She could see the bulge in my pants and said she knew I was aroused also. We sipped some more wine, and she stood and led me to her bed room and asked me to undress. I did slowly, as I removed my trousers and knit shirt, then my socks and finally my jockeys. She undressed also. I looked at her beautiful shape, bountiful breast, round butt, shapely legs, then we approached one another as we reached out and held each other as we felt each other's body. I rubbed her back before placing my hand between her legs as she parted them and felt the heat that was pent-up in her as she held my hardness in her soft hands. We stepped towards the bed and we lay down and picked up where we had left off standing. I kissed her and she kissed me back, her scent we sweet as I felt her and she parted her thighs and I rubbed her shaved vagina and felt the moisture building as she reached and held me as she erupted with a massive climax and I continued to rub her and slowly moved my hand to her breast, feeling them and rubbing a finger lightly around the aroused areola, squeezing her nipples and sending shutters through her, as I placed one between my lips and licked them.

Then I looked into her eyes as I squeezed one of her breast, before moving my hand and rubbing the inside of her thighs as shivers ran through her and moving my hand back to her vagina and rubbing it as I parted her thighs and slid down in the bed to take a closer look, parting her thighs and looking at her hot moist pussy, before spreading the lips and putting my face in between her legs and taking in the smell of perfume and sweat. I found her clit as it came out of hiding and licked it as I held her thighs and fingered her vagina as she climaxed again. I started climbing on top of her slowly licking her body as I moved up and squeezed both nipples with my mouth before kissing her and slowly inserting my hard penis into her overly hot pussy as she squirmed below me and said, fuck me please, oh please fuck me as I slid in and out and reaching around with one hand and sticking a finger up her tight rectum as she climaxed again and her juices flowed, soon her juices ran down to her ass as she moaned and I slowly pulled out and slid my hard penis up her now open and quivering ass, pumping it as she climaxed again, as I held her head with my left hand and licked her ear, as multiple orgasms filled her whole being. I came in her anus as she screamed and climaxed again as her breathing became short and ragged.

She held me with what little strength she could muster, as I rolled to her side and she turned to face me placing her head on my shoulder as I rubbed her back. I said to Renee, the last time I had sex was with my wife, and had almost forgotten how wonderful it felt. She kissed me and said that she had only masturbated since her husband's passing, but never ever had multiple orgasms before. I said I had to pee and went to use the bathroom and washed myself and my hands before returning to the bed where Renee was still laying. I climbed back in bed and she began to feel me as I laid on my back, climbing on top with me between her legs, she bent over and kissed me, biting and licking my ear and moving slowly down my body until she had me in her warm mouth and soon I was hard again as she swallowed me, she moved back up and sat on me and moved her round butt up and down before she stopped and came to another screaming climax, and laying her ample breast on my chest. She kissed me and said thank you and I held her and rubbed her back and told her how good it felt to hold her and was still inside her as she slowly moved her butt and I climaxed again this time in her and she stretched out and climaxed again, we rolled on our sides, kissed and looked at one another.

She said don't let her go, she wanted to be my lover, and started to cry as I held her. Renee said that was the best sex she had ever had, and wanted more, and wanted me. I said lets drink some wine and catch our breath and we also need to bathe. She slowly got up and took me by the hand and led me into her large bathroom, turned the water on in the walk-in shower and waited for it to get warm as we held each other. I felt her smooth body; she was in great shape for her age and didn't appear over thirty. We entered and she bathed me, and I her, she held me in her small soft hands and knelt and placed me in her mouth and it was such a great feeling, said I had to pee, she continued to kneel and said go ahead and when I did she pointed my penis at her face and when I finished she stood and I washed her face and hair. We washed one another and then we finally turned off the water and she handed me the largest bath towel ever and took one for herself.

We went to the bedroom and we oiled and massaged one another, she stood and went to her closet and came back and handed me a robe, I put it on and she put one on, took me by the hand and we returned to the living room. We took our glasses and went to the kitchen and filled them with ice and returned to the couch in the living room and poured more wine. I sat down on the couch and she laid her head in my lap. I looked down at her, and said she had made me very happy, and I was glad I had spoken to her yesterday. Told her she was very sexy, beautiful and could tell she was a sweet and loving person.

We talked about what we did with and in our everyday lives, how we felt about the world around us, and how we were going to deal with what had just happened. She asked me to spend the night with her, said that she felt like not wanting to be alone any longer. I told her I would stay the night with her, and hoped we were compatible. We drank until the bottle was empty, then she washed the glasses and cleaned up. She led me to the bed and we got in and she kissed me, and I kissed her and we felt one another and talked until we fell asleep. That was around eleven pm.

When I woke it was six am. Renee woke also, probably because of not having anyone there before. I had to use the bathroom, and several minutes later she entered and asked if I wanted some mouth wash, yes I replied and thank you, as she handed me the bottle. I asked if she didn't happen to have a spare toothbrush. She reached in the bottom cabinet and handed me a new one. I thanked her and proceeded to brush my teeth. When I finished, turned and kissed her, she hugged me and asked me to wait for her before I started to dress. I sat on the side of the bed and waited for her to come out. Several minutes later she entered and stood in front of me naked, asked me to lie in bed with her before I left, I complied and Renee said that she wanted to feel me and for me to feel her. Told me she would miss me even though we had only spent one night together, and wanted me to come back whenever I wanted. I kissed her and said I enjoyed the time spent with her and wanted to come back and spend more time with her.

I gathered my clothes and sat in a chair that was in the bedroom as she sat naked and watched me dress, I had everything on except my jacket and shoes, stood and she put a robe on and took my hand and kissed it. I walked to the living room, grabbed my jacket from the chair where I had left it and headed for the front door, slipped my shoes on, turned and Renee was standing there, she had a smile on her face. I told her that I would call her later as we reached for each other and kissed. She hugged me tight and told me to come back to her. I thanked her for the most enjoyable evening I had in a very long time and would be sure to call her later.

I walked down the stairs and went to my car, and headed home. When I arrived parked in the driveway and went in the house, to purrs and grabbed my two companions and set them on their tower and petted them before going and washing their bowls out and prepared to feed them. I changed my clothes before heading to the office.

Three

I put on my jeans and a t-shirt, running shoes and my sports jacket, checked the house before heading out. I stopped and had breakfast on the way to work, stopping at Marty's restaurant and having a breakfast of bacon and eggs with toast and coffee and a sweet roll as I sat and thought about last night. Knowing I hadn't had sex with a real woman since my wife passed, it has been quite a while, which made it hard not to feel some real compassion for the other person. When I arrived at the office, took care of the usual details and spoke to my supervisors as they brought me up to date on the daily operations and all that had happened. I in turn informed them that the sale was set for the very near future and possibly next week. Everyone knew because I had informed them a month ago when I entertained the idea of selling after I had been approached and a generous offer placed before me. I had been considering selling in my head especially after my wife passed, but one condition of the sale I insisted on was all my employees were to keep their jobs; everyone was to stay employed and had informed the union of my intentions. Everyone knew I had lost interest after my wife had passed and did there upmost to insure the operation ran as smoothly as possible, which I was very thankful for. I looked at my computer and looked for a flower delivery service, found one, called and placed an order for a mixed bouquet that included roses, and be sure they would deliver today. Gave them Mrs. Simone address, and a brief message, (thank you for a very wonderful evening).

I walked around my charter bus operation, just as six coaches were preparing to leave on a charter, checked the interiors and spoke to all the drivers. I inspected the garage and several more of the other coaches that would be leaving soon before talking to several of the mechanics and the garage foreman and the manager of operations. Then walked over to the trucking operation and spoke to the manager and the dispatcher. Business had picked up the last six months and had quite a few terminal to terminal transfers for the railroad. I walked around before I walked back to my office and again my mind was on last night. How much I missed, being with someone, especially in bed and just having someone to talk to, hold in my arms and love. It was close to lunch time and decided to go and just have a hamburger. I would cook this evening when I returned home. Didn't think I needed anything at the store, but would stop instead of going straight home. Thought I would have to return Mrs. Renee's parking placard to her very soon, and would call later and see about dropping it off. I jumped in my car and headed to the local burger shop and decided to bring it back to the office like I did many times before and eating in my office at my desk. Just when I finished eating my secretary, Mary informed me that two gentlemen from World Wide shipping were in the outer office.

They were the representatives for the future prospective buyers. I asked her to show them in as I stood when they entered. I introduced myself, and they were Mr. John Bolson and Thomas Harris. I asked them to have a seat. They complimented on how efficient my operation appeared to be and how quick deliveries were being made. I thanked them. Said they were just here to observe and see how my operation would merge into their expanding nationwide operation. Stated they hadn't seen an operation as smooth running as what they had observed here and stated it was the best they had seen of all the ones that they were considering consolidating into their operation. They stated that my operation had been looked at for several months and the way I operated was very cost effective and stated there could be a position in there company for a man with my abilities. I informed them I had built the company from scratch with my now deceased wife and had no interest in continuing in the transport business. They expressed their regrets and then asked about the office building and the property attached to it and if it was included in the sale. No, and the vacant land was part of the office. They wanted the building also and said it gave a good view of operations and soon Mr. Harris excused himself and walked to the outer office as he pulled his cell phone out and ask to speak to someone at national headquarters. He soon returned and asked how much more for the office building and adjoining parcel of vacant land next to the trucking operation. I told him $7,000,000.00 because it was energy efficient and the security was the latest. He gave the price to the person he was speaking to and told them it was worth the additional cost because of the location and the additional land adjacent to the terminal which could be used to expanded very easily. He closed his cell and said he was waiting for an answer shortly. While he waited I gave them a quick tour, showing them the backup generator, solar panels and security center, before returning to my office. He pulled out his phone and texted headquarters. Soon his phone rang and said they would buy the office building for my asking price. He stated that my attorney would be notified shortly of the additional purchase and price. They stood and said they would be back tomorrow to observe more and see what changes they would make after they acquired the properties. I shook their hands and they departed.

I sat at my desk and thought about the sale. I would receive $77,000,000.00 dollars for all my years of work. And once the charter operation was sold, I would have another $30,000,000.00 dollars. I had several real estate investments which netted me a couple million a year in income. I decided that it was time to sell my house also and make fresh start. I pulled up the RELS (real estate listing services) on my computer and entered my password. I looked at the next county over in several of the suburban areas at new and existing homes in well to do communities. Found several homes that I really liked and printed them out. I would drive by and see them before I contacted any agents. My home was out dated and small, several years old, but I kept it in shape and up to date as much as possible. I called a real estate agent friend of mine and told him I wanted to sell and to give me a time he would be available to view and list it. He said he would call me back, I said ok and would be waiting for his call. I liked the part of the Midwest where I lived, enjoyed the change of seasons, and I just really needed a fresh start and now had a great opportunity to start over and was very fortunate that all my transportation operations were being bought at the same time.

I checked my phone, I had the ringer turned off and had it on low vibrate. No calls which was good as I looked at the clock and it was close to three and decided to head home. I remembered that I needed to pick up some more cat food and would stop at Roscoe's on my way home. I didn't think about Mrs. Simone until I entered Roscoe's. I hoped she had received the flowers and note. I only needed cat food and purchased a couple dozen cans, some cat nip, and a large bag of litter, and headed for the checkout. Made my purchase and headed to my car, after placing everything in the trunk, and after getting in my phone rang. I took it out and it was Mrs. Simone, I answered. She thanked me for the flowers and told me how sweet and thoughtful it was. She asked where I was now, I said I had just stopped to pick up some cat food and litter at Roscoe's. She asked if it was the one near her home, and I said yes. Then I remembered that I needed to return her parking placard, and asked if she was home so I could return it. She said yes, and I could stop by.

I arrived shortly and parked on the street in front of her building, went inside and pressed the bell for her unit and she answered over the intercom. I was buzzed in and went up the stairs and she was standing in the door waiting. She was barefoot and wearing a thin house dress, she wore no makeup and her skin was radiant as she smiled at me, and asked me inside. After closing the door she threw her arms around me and kissed me, I hugged her rubbing her back. We released one another and I handed her the placard.

She told me, that I should keep it because she didn't want to let me go, and said I sent shivers through her, and

31

was very excited now. Said that I felt the same, but until I had completed my business transactions I was a little short on time and my attention was distracted by it. She showed me the flowers and knew I felt something for her. You are very beautiful even now, and I truly enjoyed being with you. She asked me if she could come home with me and spend the night. I was surprised by her boldness. She sensed it by my expression, and said that I had awakened her whole being and wanted to be with me. She felt that I was who she wanted to be with, even though it was just after we met. My cats might be jealous of her being in my home, sometimes it happened. I asked her if she liked cats. She thought they were cute and cuddly. I told her tomorrow would be better, it being a Saturday I wouldn't have to go to work, and we could spend the day together and see how compatible we might be. Ok and that it would work for her. I told her I liked her very much and looked forward to spending the day with her. She asked for my address and said she would drive her car to my house. We have a date then, and wrote my address on the back of another of my business cards, and handed it to her. I have to go and headed for the door. She took my hand and asked me to hold her, as I held her she whispered in my ear that she was excited and wanted me to touch her, I felt her through the thin material of her dress and she held me tight as she climaxed in my arms, I held her until she calmed down. She apologized for what had just happened and began crying and thanked me for complying with her request. Told me she never felt this way about anyone like the way she felt about me. I kissed her as she held me and told her it was alright, she didn't want to let me go. Told her I had to leave, as I opened the door and stepped out, slipped my shoes on, when I turned she started to cry again, as I said good bye and kissed her again. She closed the door and when I got to my car and looked up, she was standing at her patio door, crying with her hand between her legs.

I arrived home backing into the garage and unloaded my bags from the trunk of the car and walked across the yard to the back door. I could see Patter in the window looking outside and soon Pits was looking outside also. I opened the back door and Pits was at my feet. I came inside and placed the bags on the kitchen table, went and undressed and put on a pair of shorts and a t-shirt. I went around the house opening windows, and turned the central air off, and returned to the kitchen and put the cat food away, and checked their automated litter box, I decided to clean it completely and dumped the dirty litter into a plastic bag, then took the entire box down to the basement wash basin in the laundry room and disassembled it and sterilized the entire box, something I did once a week. Dried it, reassembled it and took it back upstairs and refilled the box with fresh litter. Went to the kitchen and made a sink full of warm dish water with bleach and whipped out their bowls and dropped them in the hot dish water, washed them and placed them in the dish rack to dry. I looked in the fridge and removed the spaghetti sauce that was made a couple days ago and took out an empty pot to boil some pasta in. After I had my dinner going, prepared to feed Pits and Patter, fixed their bowls and gave them some fresh water and placed them on their feeding stand. They ate when I ate. And they were eager to taste the food I put in their bowls; it was one that I only gave them now and then. They really loved it. I went downstairs and chose a bottle of red wine from the fridge to go with my meal. And when I returned decided it would be a nice day tomorrow to barbeque. I checked my freezer and removed a couple of steaks, some chicken, sausage, and ground beef and would make some burgers later after the meat had thawed after I had eaten dinner. My pasta was done and the sauce was almost ready, as I sat and poured a glass of wine.

I thought about Renee, she was very nice, beautiful and sexy. But was I really ready for a relationship, maybe. She was coming on strong, thinking that I should keep her at a distance for now. I know after having sex with her it broke the way I had felt, and didn't know how much I missed it until yesterday. I was more concerned with selling my businesses than anything else right now. I would have over a hundred million dollars, it was time for a real change, and I would sell this house also. Wanted something larger, less cramped, larger rooms and besides I had been here twenty two years and Sue had chosen it. I would just keep my books, some of the few accessories, pictures and give away or donate the furniture. My sauce was ready and the pasta was done so I fixed my plate, sat and began eating. I enjoyed my food, and I liked to cook, and was going to get out more and move to a more conducive neighborhood. I am not really a people person, but wanted to just start over and indulge myself, having a garden, plants and painting which I really enjoyed doing. It would be fun to have someone to enjoy it with, being by yourself isn't fun to me, but not having your own space isn't either.

I fixed my plate, and sat down to eat, blessed my food, and enjoyed every mouthful. I could understand Mrs. Simone not wanting to be alone anymore; we had wonderful sex and acted as if we didn't care about the consequences. I or we just assumed we weren't contagious and had not even discussed diseases. I had no health problems and didn't take any medications. I cleaned up and washed my plate, cleaned the pots and decided to run the vacuum through the house. I was done after about half an hour, and vacuumed the cats tower, and before I finished Patter jumped up and I ran the vacuum hose attachment over her, she enjoyed being vacuumed ever since I started doing her as a kitten, Pits came and I had to do him also, at least they were clean as I took the comb and ran it through their fur. I finished with them and replaced the vacuum cleaner bag before putting the vacuum away. I decided to take a shower since it was early evening and decided to sit out on the porch and let Pits and Patter out for a little while; they wouldn't leave the porch and usually sat together in one of the chairs or by themselves. They liked each other and sleep together if they weren't sleeping with me or in the window sunning.

I had my cell phone with the head phones on and went through it and cleared the e-mails, voicemails, and calls, and finally the text messages. Shortly after finishing I sat and looked around and could hear my neighbors mowing their lawns. Went in and grabbed a beer and returned, Pits and Patter wanted to go in the house which wasn't unusual for them as I returned and sat and sipped my beer, when my phone rang, looked and it was Renee Simone, I picked up and said hello, said that she just wanted to talk, and asked what I was doing, and went on to say that she couldn't get me out of her mind. I said you know there is a lot we haven't talked about, and one was our health. She stated that her last checkup had been two months ago, and had all the test recommended for a woman of her age, mammogram, colon ostomy, blood pressure, everything you could think of, and of course had her blood checked for any sexually transmitted diseases. I told her it has been a month since I went and had nothing wrong with me, and was glad we both were healthy. I asked her what she would be doing if she wasn't talking to me now. Said that she would probably be looking at television or knitting, and told me that there had been a couple of men who tried to ask her out but they just didn't seem her type and had declined there advances. Felt that I was special and was the reason she gave herself to me so freely and felt deep down inside I was the one for her. She wanted me to want her and hoped that I felt the same way, and knew that she was asking a lot from me in such a short time, but felt she needed to be direct with me, because that was how she felt. I told her that I appreciated her being direct, and looked forward to spending the day with her tomorrow. Then said you know, I have to prepare some burgers that I had took the meat out to thaw and needed to check on it, and need to clean the house up a little. Told her I have to go and would be very happy to see her tomorrow. She asked what time should she come. I said not before ten am, for sure because I might not be up. She missed being with me and wished she was here now, but would wait until tomorrow, good night, and said to her, to stay sweet, before hanging up.

Well I didn't expect that, and wondered about how serious she was, looked like I had a bull's eye on my back. Seems like she has made up her mind and that I was the one for her and wasn't going to stop her pursuit. Well I could have done a lot worse, I liked her and she was beautiful to look at and even better in bed, it was going to be very difficult to say no to her, and I could just feel it. I went in and chopped some veggies and made my burgers for tomorrow and placed them in an aluminum pan before placing them in the fridge. I decided to look at the news and see what the weather was going to be like. It was going to be a pleasant day, and probably a wild and exciting one for me. It was going to be another warm and humid night with rain coming soon this evening, so I went around and closed all the windows and turned the central air back on and went to the bedroom, checked my phone for some strange reason, and there was a text from Renee, it said that she felt in her heart that she loved me and would do anything I wanted, she even attached a photo of herself, at least I could use it on the contact page, it was her beautiful face and she had her makeup and lipstick on, I undressed and got in bed, pulled the covers over me and tried going to sleep as I thought about Renee and became excited, and was fully aroused and had to then relieve myself before I could go to sleep.

Four

I woke up lying in bed and felt a warm weight on my chest and there was Patter looking at me with her head down and Pits was somewhere else. I petted her as I got up and she ran off. I looked at the clock, it was almost nine as I went to the bathroom and freshened myself before going to the kitchen to make a pot of coffee, some dish water and turning the radio on to the all-news station. I cleaned the cats bowls and placed some food in there dishes along with fresh water. Made some coffee and took out the donuts and ate a couple as I sat and waited for the coffee to finish brewing, and soon pouring some in a cup and sipping the hot brew. The weather was going to be warm and sunny in the upper seventies. It was looking to be a great day ahead. I fixed a small breakfast, two poached eggs and toast and then cleaned up the kitchen. I then decided to make some potato salad, taking several potatoes out along with my other vegetables. Then turned the air conditioner off, and opened up the windows. Decided I would take a shower and afterwards applying some natural bug repellant, it smelled so very good almost like cologne. After opening the windows Pits and Patter each sat in one sunning.

I started preparing the potatoes, first peeling, slicing and soaking them before placing them on the stove to boil along with some eggs. After a short time boiling, I drained and cooled them down and as they sat and diced my other vegetables along with the boiled eggs. It wasn't long, maybe an hour later at the most before I was finished. I made sure my wine and beer was in the fridge getting the needed chill before I walked around the house looking and thinking about what would be worth keeping. I went to my office and turned on my computer and checked my e-mails and cleared them up before I brought up the RELS and scanned through available properties. I lived in a middleclass neighborhood with split level, ranch and a few bungalows, not the style of home I would be looking at in the future when I started on my trek for a new home. I would wait until I had concluded selling my business then start looking for a new residence. Knew I would eventually get a new car also since I had been driving the current one for nine years now. Didn't have much and would start over from scratch. My mind was made up, I was going to do something different and enjoy life, and the biggest question was, would I be doing it alone or not. It was ten thirty when my cell phone vibrated and I looked, and it was Renee, I didn't answer, I decided to check it and see if she left a voice message, she did, and I listened to it. Said I must be away from the phone and to call back when I received her message, there seemed to be some anxiety in her voice. Wondered if I shouldn't wait a while before returning her call, I didn't want to give the impression I was anxious. Being by yourself has advantages, but sometimes those just don't measure up to having someone in your life, but then I didn't want to appear desperate either.

I returned her call almost an hour later, and she answered right away. I said I was outside when she called and was sorry I missed it. She asked if it was alright to come now. I said sure and gave her my address, and stated she would be leaving shortly. I would be looking forward to her arrival. She asked if I needed anything. I don't think so and she could bring whatever she wanted or might need. Said she would see me soon and ended the call. I went outside and opened the umbrella, dusted a whipped off the table, cleaned the grill and placed new coals inside. I wondered how this day would turn out, really my heart was saying that maybe, Renee was the person I was to be with. But considering that I had met her and was in the mist of changing everything in my life made me wonder was this the beginning of something new, or was I moving too fast or was this the way it's supposed to happen. My wife had been older than me, and I always liked older women. Renee was a real beauty, said she was in good health which was a plus. I would just see how things worked out, one thing for sure she wasn't frigid. Sex with her was more than I could have ever asked for and she seemed compatible and compassionate, just what I needed.

I had just walked in the house when an older automobile, about as old as mine pulled into my driveway, its paint was dull and faded but it ran quietly. I looked and it was Mrs. Simone. She stepped out and I could see she was wearing shorts, with a beautiful flowered print blouse, sun glasses and a large brimmed hat, sandals with a slight heel; her legs were shapely as was her whole body. She approached the front door and rang the bell. Pits was the first to answer before I came and said good morning, and welcomed her inside. I opened the door and she entered and hugged me, kissed me and said she had missed me so very much and hadn't had a restful night since our first encounter. Pits rubbed up against her leg, and she bent over and petted him, and he seemed to enjoy her touch. I welcomed her inside and told her I had intended on grilling today and said she very much looked forward to it. I showed her around the house and she said it looked very comfortable. I said it was but had decided to sell and find something a little larger with more room inside and with a larger yard. I turned to her and said I missed you to. Said I didn't know why I felt this way, but assumed it was from being lonely for someone's company. Renee said she had thought hard about our encounter, and was scared that maybe she was letting her hormones make decisions for her and hoped she had made the right choice. I said well we seem to have come to the same conclusion and explained I had difficulty going to sleep after thinking about her and our encounter.

We went to the living room and sat on the couch together, and Pits came and wanted Renee to pet him and said he was a beautiful cat, as Patter jumped in my lap and then went over to Renee and she petted her also, and was soon purring. I said they seem to like you. Said that she liked cats better than dogs because they were so independent, unlike dogs where you had to walk them and worry about fleas and stuff they picked up from being in the outdoors. I said they don't care much for outside; they would go out on the porch and then want to come back inside after a short time. They liked her and Patter came and sat in my lap as Pits stayed in Renee's. She asked me if I could give her some advice about investments. I said to a point, and then she went on to explain that her husband had left her with a half million dollar insurance policy, and that she placed the money in a long term CD, of three years duration, the railroad accidental death policy left her with another half million, and had placed that in another CD and she was drawing his social security, her condo was paid for and only had utilities and the monthly assessment to pay. Wanted to know what to invest in or just draw interest from the accounts. I said that it would be better for her to just leave it the way it was until she could decide what she wanted to do with her life. But it didn't hurt having a stash of cash; it gave you freedom to do whatever you wanted. I said you must really feel comfortable to have told me that because the last thing you want to do is to tell a stranger about your finances. She said that was the problem she had around me, was the level of trust she felt and didn't know why she was letting herself become so vulnerable around me. I said you must really feel a sense of trust to be telling me these things and we haven't even known one another a week. Said that she could tell I was honest, fair and loving, just felt it in the way I spoke, and looked at her, and when we made love, I had taken her heart, and felt I was the best thing that had happened to her. Said she was trying hard not to admit it to herself, but she knew she loved me. Didn't expect me to feel that way, but sensed that I had some feelings for her. I told her, I didn't want to come out and say it but, I did feel that I loved her and couldn't explain how in such a short period of time, and would like to have her in my life, didn't know if it was going to be just a friendship or something more. I stood as Patter went and sat in the window and Pits followed. Renee stood and I hugged her and kissed her waiting lips. We have a lot to talk about, but first I think I need to start cooking. She asked if it was ok to bring her bag inside. I said of course and she went to her auto and retrieved a small suitcase with wheels and brought it inside. I showed her to the bedroom, where she left it. And then we went to the kitchen together.

I showed Renee what I was going to cook, and she said that was enough for the entire weekend, and asked if she had eaten anything. She had some coffee but was more excited about spending the day with me and didn't have an appetite earlier, but now could eat a little something. I made us a couple of ham sandwiches, on toasted rye, with lettuce and mustard and a pickle on the side, and a small amount of potato salad. Poured some cola in a glass with some ice and we sat down together in the kitchen and ate. She enjoyed the sandwich, and complimented me on the salad. Told her I enjoyed cooking when it wasn't a necessity and had more dishes and they all tended to be on the spicy side. Renee asked if there was anything she could do? Just relax and enjoy the day with me and that it was something I was going to start doing more of and suggested we go outside; just had to lite the grill. She asked me would I hold her before we went outside. I reached out to her and she hugged me and kissed me and said Calvino, I know I love you and it's all right if you don't feel the same way about me, but I would like to be a loving friend. I looked in her eyes and could see that she meant what she had just said to me. I ran my hand through her hair and kissed her and said I had serious feelings for her, and wanted to be sure of myself first and that she should do the same. I couldn't let our brief encounter determine the rest of our lives until we were absolutely sure that we would want to be together. Told her I felt she was the best thing that had happened to me in a long time, but didn't want my loneliness to be the reason I would be in a relationship that may prove fatal. Said she understood and probably needed to get a better hold of her feelings.

Told her it was time for me to start cooking, and we went out onto the deck and I lite the grill and waited for the fire to die down as Renee pulled a chair in the shade under the oversized umbrella and sat down. I sat and watched the fire and looked at her, she was really beautiful, her figure was a wonderful sight and she took her shoes off and I looked at her feet, she took care of herself, and any man would be proud to have her as a wife or girlfriend. I couldn't let my penis think for me, even though it was throbbing now as I admired her beautiful shape. She reached out and held my hand, it felt good not being alone, and I told her so. She said the hardest thing was the holidays being alone and said she had cried herself asleep on many nights. Didn't have anyone to hold her, kiss her, and didn't receive any gifts, flowers, or cards. Her birthday passed with no one to celebrate with. Said she knew that her loneliness was driving her to doing reckless things, like following me in the store, but felt she had to do something, couldn't take being alone any longer. Wanted some type of companionship, and lucky for her she had chosen me.

I asked her if she believed in astrology and the horoscope, somewhat she replied, but wasn't sure about it. I did, and asked for her sign; she was born in January and didn't know what signs were compatible. I said that I did and we were compatible, and I had consulted my astrology guide and told her my birthday was in October. I checked the fire and went inside and removed the pan of meats that I had prepared, bring them outside and setting them on the side board before placing them on the grill. Then lowered the top to cover them and returned and said I would be right back as I went inside and made a pitcher of punch for us to sip on. I used a bottle of red wine, grapefruit and orange juice, added some watermelon slices, pineapple, and some cantaloupe, and a half cup of Vodka. Stirred it well and filled the ice bucket with ice and took it out and placed it on the table before returning for the oversize pitcher and a couple of glasses. I added ice to the glasses, before filling both with the punch. I checked on the meats, turning them over and turned around and Pits and Patter were at the door, they smelled the food and I let them outside. They were polite and climbed into the empty chairs in the sun and stretched out. They didn't mind Renee being here which really surprised me; maybe they missed having a woman around.

They had clowned when Sue's sister stayed after she had passed away and had asked for some of her things. I kept her bath robe and some of her jewelry, but that was it. I donated most of her things to the church. Renee said the punch was really good. She asked me if I didn't mind if she went inside and changed into her swim suit, I said go right ahead. She stood and I asked if she needed a robe before she went into the house, said she had brought one and thanked me. Five minutes later she returned wearing one of those thong suits. It just covered her nipples and crotch, she was a real beauty and wasn't afraid to let me see her. She said to me that she had never worn it before, but since I had seen her nude, didn't think I would mind. Said I sure don't as long as you're not offended by me just staring at such a wonderful sight. I told her she was making it difficult not to want her. She said that's good because it's what she wanted more than anything else. She had a light summer robe with her as she placed it in the chair and began to rub olive oil on herself from a small bottle. Told her I was glad I had met her, and was starting to have palpitations from her presence. I went inside and got my phone and returned and took some candid photos of Renee before I asked her to pose for several which she did without hesitation. I then left and returned to the grill and turned my meats over to check they weren't cooking to fast. My neighbors came out onto their deck and we spoke briefly. We exchanged some small talk as they left to start their grill also. I know they were curious and wanted to see who I had over since no one had been here since my wife passed. I noticed them especially Mr. Johns looking over and trying to get a good look at my visitor.

I said to Renee, you know I told you I that I'm selling my businesses and I am going to sell this house, and eventually buy myself a new auto. I have been here more than twenty years, if my neighbors knew my net worth I probably wouldn't be safe. I must and intend to start a new life and didn't know if meeting you was the start of it or not. I had always been attracted to older women; my wife was older than myself, same as you. I feel surer of myself now and I am ready for that change, and hope you are a part of it. I have a friend and will let him sell this house for me, and once I close on the business maybe next week I will start   looking for a new house. Will probably move out and have everything cleaned up, repaired and painted and other than my books and some small stuff I was going to purchase all new furniture. I don't know what you do during the day but would probably welcome your company. She was listening as she oiled herself and asked me to do her back as she came over and sat in my lap, I generously applied the oil to her and massaged her as she began to moan and said she loved the way I felt on her. I told her I liked feeling on her also. Pits and Patter had enough sun and when I finished with Renee they were waiting at the back door wanting to go inside. I opened the back door and they scampered inside as I went to refill the ice bucket. Renee followed me inside, and asked me to please hold her, I held her briefly and said I have to watch the food, and returned shortly to check my meats. I had a pan and began removing the sausages and checked the chicken and they were finished cooking also, and not overdone, as I turned over the remaining burgers, and closed the lid. Renee returned with her sun hat and put on her robe, as I poured myself some more punch. I wanted her, but was trying not to reveal my feelings too soon, felling real comfortable around her, like I had known her more than just the four days since we met. Didn't know what was happening to my feelings and looking at her didn't help as my penis throbbed, as I tried hard to suppress any sexual thoughts that I had. I checked on the burgers and they were finished cooking, removed them and closed up the grill so I could reuse the coals again.

I told Renee that she could eat if she wanted. Said she wasn't hungry yet and would wait. Ok. She asked me what locations I was looking at for a new home to be located. Said I just started looking, and had seen several that appealed to me, but wasn't certain yet since I had just began to look and was really waiting until I had concluded all my business. Then all my time would be mine, my obligations would be at a minimum and would only have my real estate operations to watch over and they weren't a problem since they were more on the industrial side and had long term leases. Renee said she would like to be with me when I started looking and asked if that would be ok with me. Said I would welcome her being with me, and would value her opinion and would probably be riding around and looking at different areas and neighborhoods first before I did any real in-depth searches.

Renee said it was difficult for her being a widower and not having anyone to talk to, and said I bet you talk to Pits and Patter a lot, and could tell that they loved me, and only a caring person would have animals in their life and could tell by their condition that you take good care of them. I said it was time we ate something and was going to make us a couple of plates and asked her to join me. We went inside to the kitchen and took out a lettuce I had cleaned earlier and pulled off some leaves and placed them in a plate and dished some potato salad on top, then handed her a plate and asked her what meats she wanted and we both had a piece of chicken and a sausage. I placed condiments on the table and some toasted buns, then the silver ware. But said first I have to fix Pits and Patters bowls. I washed their bowls, before preparing their food, mixing some dry with some can before placing their bowls on the stand and washed out their water bowl and refilled it, placing some ice in it. They eagerly ate, and told Renee they ate when I did, and had read when you use the self-feeders they tend to become overweight and that wasn't good for their health.

We sat down and after blessing our food, enjoyed it and each other's company. It had gotten much warmer than they said it would be which wasn't bad since I had watered my plants the day before. I said air conditioning was fine but didn't mind the house being a little warm as long as it wasn't extremely hot. Renee said she liked the warm weather especially after winter. Told her I liked the change of seasons and people who lived there were healthier than living in a warm climate all the time. She liked the change also. We ate and Renee said the food was very good and she would love to cook for me someday. You may get your chance sooner than expected. She asked what I meant by that, I said you told me you wanted to be with me, so if you're with me someone has to cook, I am not a restaurant person, only by necessity. I like to know where my food comes from and that it's clean, that's why there is so many outbreaks related to food, not being cleaned or under cooked, or the workers not adhering to sanitary rules. She agreed with me and liked to eat at home but wanted most of all to eat and sleep with someone because being alone was no fun and especially now since she had met me. When we finished I washed our dishes and we went back outside on the deck as the sun slowly went down. We finished our punch. Soon it was getting dark as we went inside and turned on the television and looked at the late news. I was more concerned about the weather, and we were in for some storms overnight. We sat close, I had my arm around her shoulder, I smelled like smoke and meat and said to Renee that I needed to shower; she still had her thong bathing suit on.

I told her that I had a hard on all day from looking at her. Said she was trying hard to control herself also. Based on the weather I needed to close and lock the windows and turn the central air back on. And so I went around and secured the house, turned the central air on and came back, took her to the bedroom and closed the door since Pits and Patter were elsewhere so we wouldn't have to worry about them disturbing us. The bath was right there and I had a walk-in shower also. we undressed each other and I smelled her sent and kissed her like I hadn't seen her in years, pushed her to the bed, reached for her foot and stuck a toe in my mouth as she squirmed and reached up and pulled her thong down spreading her legs, and climbed in between them, spreading them apart and taking in the clean warm sent of her, spreading her vaginal lips and looking at her clit as she became more aroused as she moaned. I placed a finger inside of her, then licked her sweetness, placed my tongue on her clit as she became wet with perspiration and climaxed as I continued to lick all around her vagina, before climbing slowly up to her ample breast, and moving aside the small patches of cloth of her suit and placing an aroused nipple in my mouth, as she reached down to remove my shorts with some difficulty as I moved to the other breast and squeezed the nipple in my mouth between my lips. We stopped and removed our clothes and picked up where we had left off. I placed my left arm under her head and my right leg between hers as I held her and rubbed her back and butt cheeks. I squeezed her cheeks as she kissed me, and asked her if she was going to be a good girl, and smacked her butt, she held me and said yes sir, I smacked the other as she began to climax again and felt her from behind. She asked that I spank her again, I smacked her butt several more times and then felt between her legs feeling her and then lightly smacking her vagina several times as I whispered in her ear that she had been naughty and its why she was being punished as she erupted in a massive climax as I held her tight, and played with her clit, feeling inside her, as she screamed yes, please I will be good. I waited for her to calm down some as I climbed on top of her parting her legs and telling her I was going to fuck her sweet pussy and slowly began to insert myself as she screamed fuck me hard, I did and she was ecstatic as she climaxed again, and begged me not to stop, and said use her, fuck her, and she climaxed again, I pulled out and told her to turn over and she did as she was told, to get that ass up and I fucked her from behind as I reached around and played with her clit, as another organism racked her body, then I pulled out and parted her ass cheeks and slowly worked it in her anus as she screamed and climaxed as I played with her clit, I was deep in her ass when I came and had a massive climax, before I slowly pulled out. When I was out she collapsed on the bed.

She slowly rolled over and reached out for me as I lay next to her and held her tight. Telling me she loved me and started crying. I held her and rubbed her quivering body all over for several minutes before I said to her we needed to shower. I rose and pulled her up and when she was standing, held her tightly, rubbed her and felt between her legs and told her if she wanted to be with me I liked to play games to keep it exciting and asked if she's up for it, she shook her head yes, since she was still choked up with tears. I could tell she would do anything I wanted just to be with me as I walked her to the bathroom, turned on the water, when it was warm led her into the shower and took the soap, lathered her up playing with her ass and pussy. I pressed her against the wall and made her climax again, told her she was mine now, holding her with one arm and placing my leg between hers and spanking her ass as she climaxed again, and said yes. She bathed me and I took the enema bag and filled it with hot water and stuck it up her butt. She had to go sit on the toilet afterwards. She returned and I played with her anus and when I had to pee she knelt down and I gave her a golden shower, and told me I had blessed her as we bathed a long time before we came out. I placed a large towel around her and took one for myself. I dried her off and she did me and we returned to the bedroom. I laid out my towel, took some massage oil and massaged her limp body from head to toe, front and back. She was so beautiful lying there; I laid next to her and held her, and said that was the best sex I had ever had, that she excited me so much. She held me and she wanted to massage me. She started with my back and when she finished I turned over she began again, and when she reached my crouch used her soft hands to make me hard again and bent down and placed her mouth around me, I asked her to turn around while she did me, as she did and I pulled her crotch toward my face and soon had her sweet pussy and ass in my face as I licked her and she climaxed again, she turned around and sat on me, then laid down on me with her ample breast, and kissed me and I kissed her back. I was inside her and she felt good, as she whispered in my ear that she belonged to me, would do anything I wanted, that she loved me and knew for sure I was the one for her, and please would I take her with me wherever I go from this day forward. I rolled her over to her side and held her and kissed her. I started to speak and she placed a finger to my lips, and she said don't speak now. We just held one another and I felt her as we both calmed down.

Renee, sweetheart let's have a drink. We need to remember this very special moment. Do you have any sweat pants, said she had brought a set. Why she asked, the cats might want to climb on you and I wouldn't want you to get scratched up, they still had their claws. I pulled out a clean pair from the closet, as she removed hers from her overnight bag. After we had dressed I took her in my arms and held her. Told her I loved her and that she was growing on me. I released her and opened the door and no cats. I took Renee downstairs to the basement bar and fixed us a couple of Martinis. We sat on the couch and I turned on the radio. We held each other, she told me the sex we had was like nothing she had ever experienced. Told her I hadn't either and maybe it was a sign that we were to be together as we sipped the martinis. I said to her I really preferred a gin and tonic, we finished and I fixed us a couple more. I came and sat next to her before Pits appeared and climbed on our laps, licking both our hands and then lying in Renee's lap, Patter soon appeared and climbed on the back of the sofa behind my neck licking it and purring. Soon after we finished our drinks and headed to bed.

We pulled the cover back as we both sleep in the nude and it was a great feeling as we pulled the covers up over us and Pits lay at the foot of the bed and Patter laid in the chair. I was glad they were being hospitable towards Renee. We held each other and spoke of the future. I asked her what she thought would happen now. Said life isn't a fairy tale; we have both experienced the bad things that can happen when you lose someone you love and have been with a long time. She loved her husband but he was away more than he was home, and after the accident she realized just how alone it would be for her and thought that she could live alone but after a while the things she desired most money couldn't buy, trust, honesty, companionship and a caring love. That's why she had dressed up and walked to the store when we met, decided to see if anyone noticed her or cared, that's when she noticed me. Said I was hansom and gave out a vibe that just felt positive to her and decided to see when she approached me and asked for my help, and when I had complimented her, felt just maybe we could be friends. And when I asked her out to dinner she was surprised at how cordial I was. Just took a chance based on her feelings, and lucky for her I didn't turn out to be a pervert or a rapist. She was scared now that she thought about how stupid it was what she had done. Said I was glad it was me also, because you have given me more of a reason to press ahead with my plans now. She asked what plans. I said you will see if what you said is true. Renee said she was true to her word, wanted to be with me no matter what. We hugged and rubbed each other until we fell asleep.

Five

We woke and it had rained most of the night, we hadn't heard a thing. Pits and Patter were walking around the house and came in and lay on my chest and on Renee. I got up and went to the bathroom and freshened myself, before returning to the bedroom. Renee was just waking up and Pits was purring and laid next to her head, she woke and petted him, then sat up, and I said good morning baby. She smiled and got up and hugged me and went to the bathroom. Did you sleep well? It was the best sleep since we sleep together the last time she said, as we put on our sweat pants and headed to the kitchen.

I first started coffee and then made some dish water and took Pits and Patters bowls and washed them out and decided to give them some dry food with their fresh water and checked their litter box. I cleaned it before returning to the kitchen and washed my hands again. I poured Renee and myself some coffee and had some coffee cake, before I started breakfast. Renee asked if she could fix the breakfast. Sure as I took out the pans, eggs, bacon and bread. She asked do you want onions or cheese. Cheese toast would be ok as I removed a package of sliced mozzarella from the fridge. Renee was a good cook and soon we were sitting down eating. Pits and Patter were happy now and ran around the house before climbing on their tower. We finished eating and I cleared the table and washed the dishes.

Checking the temperature, I decided to open the windows, turned the air off and opened the house up. Went to the bed room and started making up the bed as Renee followed me and helped. When we finished I suggested we go for a walk, I grabbed my keys and we left out the front door and walked around the neighborhood, we walked our food down and a little more than half hour later returned. I asked her if she remembered our conversation yesterday, she responded yes, and would never forget it. I slipped my hand under her shirt and felt her as she looked me in my eyes and said she belonged to me and was mine. She reached and pulled her shirt up and then mine saying, make love to me. We undressed and our hands were all over each other, soon she was sitting on top of me as we came together and just laid there holding each other as we kissed.

It was such a lovely day we decided to relax outside on the deck, we had our lounge chairs next to one another and we talked. I asked are you happy and how do you feel about yourself. She told me that the anxiety had eased up and just wanted to start on my adventure with me, and that she had no commitments or obligations and would give anything to be with me. Renee, I'm happy and I would take you on my adventure because I would rather not be alone, and felt two was always better than one. The sun had come up and wanted to take a nap and just felt a needed to relax and asked her to come inside with me. We went in and lay on top of the bed as we talked and looked at each other closely before falling asleep together again.

It was mid-day when we awoke. Pits was lying at my head, he was asleep also as I listened to him purring. He stretched out as he moved to lie between us and was happy to be there. Renee petted him and asked me how soon would it be before I really began to start looking and packing. Hopefully by the end of the week, but that wasn't a given. Now I was beginning to get anxious about it because she was here, and all I thought I would do. I was glad she was here to at least give me another opinion about the things I would be planning to do. She asked how much money I would receive when I sold my business. Some millions, as she sat up and looked at me, her mouth was open, as she was speechless. She said all this time, you have been working and building your business, not enjoying life, lonely, with just your cats, don't you know that you deserve to start over, you have been blessed and you need a change and a real chance to be happy. Said she understood now when I said yesterday, if your neighbors knew you wouldn't be safe. Yes you must move, and I will make sure you do. Told me I could stay with her, and that way I could have my house cleaned and painted, and would help me with anything and everything I needed done. She reached out and hugged me and told me, I needed her more than I knew.

Renee said to me it wasn't money she wanted from me but my love, and was just curious, she wasn't needy and didn't need anything but my love and companionship and money couldn't buy that. She wanted to love me and just be with me. She kissed me and now wanted to eat some of the food we had fixed yesterday. We went and prepared ourselves a couple plates, and then we sat and ate. When we finished I went and fixed Pits and Patters bowls. When they finished eating placed them on their tower and combed them out and then they were happy. Renee asked me if she could spend another night. I told her it wasn't going to be a request any longer, that we had committed ourselves to one another unofficially, and I would accept her offer of residence. Said she was glad that I would and hugged me as we then decided to fix some drinks and sit outside on the deck. We talked as the sun went down and then went inside and watched some television and were soon joined by the cats and each chose a lap to sit in. we watched several shows and Renee said she would go home when I left for work tomorrow, we petted Pits and Patter until they left one by one. After the news was over we went to the bed room and made sweet love before taking a long shower together where we had more sex. Afterwards we oiled each other and I slipped on my robe and secured the windows and turned the air conditioning on again. As I returned, found Renee was under the covers waiting for me. I crawled into bed with her and we hugged and kissed and said good night and went to sleep holding one another.

Six

I woke early around six and proceeded to the bathroom, washed and prepared for the day ahead. Renee was still asleep as I looked upon the person I was falling in love with, or rather had fallen in love with and was going with me onto the next phase of my life. I knew this was going to be a happy friendship even if it didn't turn out to be a close relationship. I headed for the kitchen and made the coffee and took out the coffee cake. Made dishwater and did my usual morning ritual for my feline friends. They were straight for the day as I returned and checked on my house guest just as she turned over and felt for me. She rose and I said good morning love, she returned the greeting as she stretched. It was a beautiful sight just looking at her as she stood and came to me and I hugged her before she went to the bathroom to freshen up. When she returned after putting her robe on, we hugged again, running her fingers through my hair as we kissed, and as we did she said that she would miss me since it was Monday and we had to start our week. Told her I would miss her very much also.

We went to the kitchen and I poured her a cup of coffee and we sat and I said that I hoped that everything went smoothly because now that I knew her, my life had new meaning. She agreed with me, and said she would go to her part time job and resign and return and clean her house and make some room for me. We finished our coffee and she asked about breakfast. I told her that would be nice if she wanted to fix it but I usually stopped on the way to work. She insisted that I eat before leaving and I should start getting use to someone caring about me. I thanked her and said I needed a real change. She prepared the meal as we then sat and ate as I told her how I appreciated her concern. I cleaned up as she left to dress. It wasn't long before we were both ready to depart. She had her bag ready by the door as I checked the house and we hugged and kissed. She insisted that I call her sometime today and said she loved me as we departed. I helped her to her car and put her bag inside for her and we kissed again. She backed out the driveway and I went to the garage and got into my car and headed for work.

I arrived at work and headed to my office and looked over the weekend paper work as my supervisors gave there reports and said everything had gone smoothly as usual which was good news. At about ten I received a call from my attorney, he said both sales were set for Wednesday and I should have a new account for the money to be transferred to. Ok and would take care of it today. He also stated both sales would be at the same bank, and he gave me the name of the bank and advised me it would simplify things if I opened an account there. It would be at ten and eleven in the morning and that possession would occur at that time. A written guarantee would be given retaining all employees. I thanked him and called my secretary into the office and asked her to call the union representatives and stewards together for a meeting tomorrow at ten o'clock. I called the union offices and spoke to both the local presidents and said my secretary would call to confirm, they knew I was going to sell and regretted my decision but understood my reasons, and said they would be with me at the closing. I went to the outer office and pulled a bankers box from the storage closet, returned and unfolded the box and started packing my personal belongings. I would miss being here but it was time to go on with my life.

I informed my secretary that I would return before the day was over and headed for the bank. It was American Central and went to the main where the sales would take place and filled out the appointment book and had a seat until I was called. Once I explained to the representative my purpose, he picked up the phone and shortly the vice president of the bank came, shook my hand and asked me to come with him, we went to his office and he knew of the pending sale that was to occur as I opened and account for the transfer of funds. I would have to make a deposit into the account and transferred funds from one of my real estate corporate account in the amount of $10,000.00. He asked for a second name on the account, I gave him Mrs. Renee Simone as the second name. She was the best thing that had happened to me, and I didn't have anything to loose and no close relatives. Once that was completed, headed for lunch at a hot dog shack that had the best hot dogs in town, I ate there before returning to the office.

Soon packing the few things I thought I wanted which wasn't much, it didn't even fill the box, just a few pictures and some books I kept. I understood my operating accounts would be reimbursed in the sale and made notes of the balances. It wasn't long before the day started coming to an end. My friend Tommy Jones called and asked when he could see the house and run some comps. This evening would be fine and said he would come by between five and six. Ok and would see him latter. I told my secretary I was gone for the day and would see them all tomorrow as I departed.

When I arrived home, parked in the driveway, opened the garage so Tommy could look inside when he arrived. Went inside and opened up the house since the temperature was about seventy outside. I fed my cats and went and changed clothes. Put on shorts and a t-shirt and called Renee. She wasn't home and I left a message on her answering machine. Warmed the last of the grilled food, took a bottle of wine from the fridge and after a while sat down and began to eat. When I finished, cleaned up and waited for Tommy.

Tommy showed up a little after five pm and looked the house over and said I had really kept it in good shape and up to date. I was willing to take out a seller's insurance policy that covered the appliances and house mechanicals for up to a year after the sale. He looked up on his laptop and came up with some comps for a three bedroom two and a half bath house in the area and it was around $295,000.00 and said that we would start there. I was going to first move out and have everything painted inside and the carpets cleaned. He asked me how soon. I replied as soon as I had emptied the house of the all the furniture. He went around and measured the rooms and wrote down everything pertinent about the house, the new windows, roof a year old, new central heat and air, two and a half car garage, and the lot size. While he was filling out his papers, Renee called. Told her Tommy was here looking at the house and I would call her back, and said I missed her. Said she missed me also. Tommy finished and I asked him to wait until I had moved out before listing the house, he stated that wasn't a problem. I signed the exclusive listing agreement and he shook my hand and departed.

I called Renee back and she asked me about my day. Explained what had happened and all would be settled Wednesday, and I would pick up boxes and tape tomorrow on my way home. She told me she had resigned from her part time job and was going to spend tomorrow cleaning up and making some room for me. I thanked her and said the litter box could go in the second bathroom. Said she would help me pack if I wanted her assistance. I would welcome it. She asked me if I had eaten yet. Said yes, had ate the remaining food from the weekend, and would spend time deciding what I would keep, and that wasn't going to be very much. She wanted to come over but then said I wouldn't get anything done and would do what she had to do there. Told me to be careful and maybe call her before she went to bed, said she missed me and loved me and to stay safe, then our conversation ended.

I fixed Pits and Patters bowls. Afterwards went and placed all I was going to pack in the middle of the floor. I would keep my books, and my mother's photos which were still in boxes from when she passed away. I would take the few clothes I owned, the cat tower and there stuff, and my pots and pans, mixing bowls and some of my favorite glasses. There wasn't much in the basement, just the bar and our old fridge. Of the other bed rooms, one was empty an old bed room set was in the other. That along with the one I slept on I would donate. Decided that I would order one of those containers they bring to your home, you load it up and they bring it to where ever when you are ready. I just needed my clothes and Pits and Patters stuff. When I finished, was surprised at how little I really had after all these years. Had given Sue's family a lot of stuff after she passed and she had some nieces and nephews who probably would come and clean me out if I offered. I would give her sister a call and see. I called Sue's sister and told her I was moving and if she or any of the family wanted anything, they could come get it this coming weekend and could have all the furniture in the house, it was good furniture but had made up my mind to start over and it didn't make sense to move somewhere and then you ended up getting rid of stuff because it didn't fit or didn't fit the decor. Said she would come with her daughter and son in-law and her son, said they could always use furniture. Said she would call in a couple days and let me know when. She thanked me for thinking of them; they lived about eighty miles away and would make a day of it.

It had gotten late, checked the house and locked up before I took my shower and climbed in bed alone, really missing Renee. I called her and said I was in bed and wished her a good night, she thanked me for calling and I would talk to her more tomorrow.

Seven

The following morning, the day began as it has the past several years. As I thought about the day that was about to unfold, I would be speaking to my employees, except this would be the last time and would be one of the most unforgettable moments in my life. I had made my morning coffee and took care and fed my furry friends before I left home, petted them and told them things were about to change. They looked at me like they really understood, as I left and locked the door behind me. I stopped and had breakfast, this would probably be one of the last times I would be eating here, as I finished and left a generous tip. After arriving at the office I checked everything as I usually do and received the overnight reports and looked them over and then prepared to meet with the union officials, shop stewards and employees at both operations, it would be short and brief. Everyone began arriving and I greeted them and we soon headed for the loading and transfer dock. With the union officials I shook their hands and we first went to the trucking operation and made an announcement over the public address system and had all the employees gathered that were there, came to about twenty-five, some were on the road. Everyone knew before today I was going to sell and I addressed them and thanked them for their loyal support over the years and that I had negotiated their job security into the sale and their union president thanked me as they all wished me well. I shook everyone's hand and then we, the union officials and I walked over to the charter bus service operation. I did the same thing again, and most was sorry to see me go. I then returned to my office and the union representatives thanked me and said they would be at the sale tomorrow. I left early after thanking my office staff, and headed home. There was no reason for me to stay any longer since my involvement was basically over at this point.

I stopped on my way home at the Self Haul rental and purchased a couple dozen boxes of various sizes, along with some packing tape. I headed home and when I arrived placed the boxes inside, and then went to the garage and looked around, there wasn't anything here I wanted either. I returned to the house and hung up my jacket and after feeding my cats, started to pack, with my books being first, when I finished with them I only had seven small heavy boxes, packed my movies and music two more boxes, taped and sealed them and labeled them. Set them to one side and added my mother's three boxes to the pile on one side of the living room, and felt that was enough for the day. And decided I would do a little at a time before deciding to place the photos that I wanted to keep in a box, that wasn't much. Checked my office, there wasn't much, except for my computer, printer and speakers. I would leave them for last. Looking in all the kitchen cabinets; there wasn't much food, mostly for the cats, which was good. Looked in the fridge and it was much the same, mostly fresh veggies and only a few. Well this would be easy. Decided to go out and get some fried chicken and returned in about forty minutes, sat and ate, what I didn't eat, I cleaned the meat off the bone and chopped it up and put it in the cats bowl, they were very happy and purring. I decided to retire early and took a nice long hot shower. When I came out putting on my shorts and t-shirt and it was around seven, when the doorbell rang.

I went to the door and it was Renee. Opened the door for her and we held each other. I had missed her call and besides she wanted to be with me, she had her purse and a large beach bag. Told me she was going to spend the night. She looked around and saw I had been busy. Told her I had showered and was going to bed early. She said not without her. I asked her if she had eaten, said she had. Good because Pits and Patter finished the leftovers. I fixed us some drinks and we relaxed on the deck. Told her tomorrow was the big day and Tommy had looked at the house and I would have one of those containers delivered and place what I was keeping inside it. We finished, I locked up as we went inside, cleaned up and we went to bed. We didn't have sex, instead she gave me a massage and I went to sleep. I woke up briefly later and went to the washroom, returned and she was sound asleep. My beloved cat, Pits was in the chair and Patter was at the foot of the bed, as I dosed off again.

Eight

We woke up together, we kissed, went to the bathroom together, we freshened up and I put on my shorts and robe. Renee put what she had worn over on and we went to the kitchen and I made some coffee. She looked in the fridge and at least I still had bacon and eggs, and bread. She began fixing breakfast and soon we were sitting and eating together. I thanked her for the massage. She said I needed it and would be getting them more often. She reached and held my hand, and said everything was going to be alright. I fed the cats and cleaned their box and then we cleaned up the kitchen and then went to get dressed, after removing my robe Renee came and held me, kissed me as we held each other. Said to call her when I was ready to move my clothes and the cats and she had plenty of closet space and the little bit of food I had left would not be a problem. I dressed and she went to the porch and started combing Patter and Pits, they liked her and purred and both wanted to be combed, and Renee combed them both. I finished dressing and wore a suit for today, and would be glad when it was all finally over.

I closed up and turned the air on and Renee and I walked out together. I opened the car door for her and before she got in we kissed and then she was gone. I got into mine and drove to the office for the very last time. I arrived and greeted everyone and checked my operating accounts, and made a note of the amounts and finished placing the few remaining mementos in the box, took one last look around and shook hands as I departed with my box in hand. I got in my car and headed directly to the bank, sat in the parking lot and thought about myself and how fortunate or foolish my decision today was going to turn out. One thing for sure with a hundred million dollars in the bank I should be able to do anything I wanted. I got out of the car and walked inside the bank and headed to the executive offices and checked in. I had just started to have a seat when the receptionist asked me to follow her and led me to a conference room. When I entered my attorney and the union officials were already seated and the buyers were soon following me in as I entered the large conference room. There was a CPA and a closer from the title company, attorneys for the buyer, and a representative for the buyer and myself. The meeting was started and I only had to sit back and listen as the transfer of assets was made. I signed several documents, relinquishing ownership and after forty minutes the transfer of funds was made. The bank verified the transfer and I signed a receipt for the final sale then the operating funds, then the deed for the office property. At the conclusion of the sale I received $78,865,571.14. My attorney and some of the union officers and I took a break before the sale of my charter bus operation.

It wasn't long before the other buying party showed up and I and my attorney and several of the union officials reentered the conference room. The transfer went smoothly, and again, transfer of the garage and rolling assets were made. Again I signed over title to the land and building and was handed a check which I endorsed and then another one for my operating accounts. This sale netted me $30, 987,660, 98 dollars. The bank verified the transfer. We all shook hands and departed. Well it had gone without a problem and my attorney handed me a bill for $175,000.00. I went and had a cashier's check drawn and paid him. I had taken care of all the loose ends and now had $109,678,232.12 dollars, and that didn't include my real estate accounts which I knew had more than five million. I then headed home.

I went home and pulled out my secure brief case and placed my account information and papers inside and spun the combination. Undressed and changed before going to my home office, and called the painter, and asked for him to come by and give me an estimate some time tomorrow. I called Renee and told her everything had gone as planned and I would like to go to lunch with her, and said I would see her in an hour, she said ok, and told her I would be wearing jeans. I checked that Pits and Patters had fresh water. They came to their tower when I stood by it with the comb in hand. I combed them and then looked at both and told them, we were moving; they looked at me, just like they understood, rubbed them both and washed my hands before heading out.

When I arrived at Renee's condo I parked out front and went in and buzzed her bell. Said it was me and walked up the stairs to her unit and she was waiting on me. She hugged me and said she was ready, handed me the guest placard for parking and told me to just keep it. She locked her door and we went to Sea World restaurant. I decided on steak and lobster and she ordered the same. I ordered two glass of wine, and said I feel a weight has been lifted off my back as she held my hand, and I looked at her. Our food came and I really enjoyed it more this time than in the past. I told her the sale went smoothly, and I had called a painter for and estimate, and my deceased wife's sister and family was to take whatever they wanted this weekend. But I wanted to move Pits and Patter and myself out before then, and some of the stuff I was keeping. The cube was coming later today and I would load it up then. Renee said that sounds like a plan and should go smoothly and she would help me with packing, and loading the cube. We finished and said I would take her home later and we could start packing things up. I thanked her for her assistance as we headed to my house.

We arrived and five minutes later the cube truck arrived. I had parked on the street and he dropped it in the driveway just in front of the garage. He handed me the information and stated just call the day before for a pickup. He left and Renee and I began packing. I had a stack of newspaper for wrapping my pots and cookware. I wasn't taking any dishes, would just shop for some new ones, for once I was going to purchase whatever I wanted. It only took a couple hours, and we were through with packing and I took the old hand truck from the garage and wheeled the boxes into the cube. I decided I would take my computer to Renee's condo since she had internet and Wi-Fi and used a small laptop. She also suggested I take my computer, the cats and my clothes today, and we would finish up tomorrow. I agreed with her and we loaded up my car and I Place Pit and Patter in there carrier and made the first trip of the day to our new temporary home. We made two more trips later that day and I was basically moved out. I had my papers and documents, Pits and Patter and there stuff, my clothes and personals. I made one final trip to secure the house and garage and the cube. I returned to Renee's condo tired, she had given me a set of keys, and told me welcome home lover.

We showered together and we oiled one another and when we finished and got in bed she massaged me and that was all I remembered. I woke up early and went to the bathroom and found my toothbrush, and freshened myself. When I returned found Renee still asleep and looked for Pits and Patter, found Pits in the second bed room and found Patter on the tower sleep. Found their bowls and food and washed them and fixed them up. Returned to the second bathroom and cleaned there litter box, before returning to where Renee was, and climbing back in bed with her, it was six and I knew she was tired after all we had done the day before. I rubbed her and she began to moan and shortly after turned over waking and reaching out for me. I continued rubbing her and shortly we were embracing each other as our passions started to rise. Soon we were having sex and after we came together lay holding one another again. We got up and showered together before putting on some shorts and t-shirts and making breakfast. She did everything and told me welcome home. She opened the patio curtains and door and the air felt good and fresh as I stepped out on the porch. Pits came out and looked around and then left and wanted to go back inside and climbed onto his tower. I felt comfortable here with her and said so as we sat down and ate. The more I looked at her, the more I loved her and knew in my heart what I would eventually do. I would hold out a little longer before I just couldn't.

Renee asked what I was going to do today and said I was going back to the house because the painter was coming to give me an estimate. It wasn't long before he called and asked me what would be a good time; I looked at the clock and said to him nine. He stated he would be there. I informed Renee; and she suggested we finish packing and bringing the rest of my clothes over. I agreed with her, and that is just what we did. We dressed and headed to my soon to be former residence. We finished packing the remaining boxes with what was going into the cube. I only packed some towels and wash cloths, the newer stuff, and loaded up the car. The painter had come while we were there and given me and estimate of $1200.00 dollars. My former sister in law called and said they would be coming tomorrow with a truck. I told her good, that she could have anything that was left, and she would need a large truck and asked her to take everything, she said it wasn't a problem, and would see me tomorrow before noon. Renee and I locked up and headed to her home. A few trips later and we were really tired, and we went out to eat again.

When we returned, went and opened a bottle of wine and sat and talked, looked at some news as Pits and Patter came and sat in our laps. I talked to them and they realized that we had moved and I was with them as they moved from me to Renee's laps as we sat and petted them. Then I realized they wanted to be fed, I fixed their bowls and we didn't see them anymore. Renee had a desk and I hooked up my computer and made sure it was working and updated it. It had gotten late and I was ready for bed. We went and showered and Renee and I massaged each other before we crawled under the covers and fell asleep.

The next morning I washed up, returned and slipped my shorts on, went to the kitchen and made some dishwater and fixed Pits and Patters bowls. When I finished checked their litter box, dumped the waste and finished. Washed my hands and looked at the clock, it was close to seven and returned to bed and laid back in bed with Renee. I rubbed her beautiful body and used some of the oil that was in the headboard. She was sleeping soundly as I rubbed her and soon she was moaning and slowly turned over as I continued rubbing her and soon she woke and spoke. I said good morning love, as she rose to use the bathroom. She returned and got back in bed. I rubbed on her some more and soon I brought her to a rousing climax, and continued to rub her as I held her and she climaxed a second time. I let her catch her breath as I held her and said I loved her and thanked her for being in my life. Said I was getting up because I had a full day ahead of me.

We rose and dressed and she prepared for us a beautiful breakfast. Afterwards I suggested she stay here today, as I left to meet my former in-laws. Said she needed to clean up and arrange things and hang my clothes up. Asked me if I would pick up a few things at the grocery and she would fix dinner, said it was time for a home cooked meal. I said thank you and she handed me a short list. I would pick it up on my way back. I prepared to leave and started on my way out when she grabbed me, kissed and hugged me, told me to be safe. I kissed and held her and told her all I wanted to do now was be here or where ever with her, that I felt a real joy in my heart that I hadn't felt in a very long time. I headed out as she locked the door behind me.

I arrived and pulled next to the pod container in the driveway. My neighbor came out to talk to me, asked me if I was moving and said, yes I was. And was getting the house prepared for sale. Said he was sorry I was moving and wished me luck. I thanked him and went back inside. I walked around and there wasn't anything else I wanted. The pod only had boxes inside. Sue and I had lived a simple life and we had said one day we would decorate the house; we had never gotten around to it. I liked art and just never had the time, neither one of us. Now maybe I can fulfill the dreams I always had. Just sorry she wasn't here for this day, well anyway things happen and life goes on. I laid down on the couch and soon dosed off. I must have sleep a little more than an hour when I had to get up to pee. I returned and the next thing I know this large rental truck backs into the driveway, and I look out and a car pulls up and parks and its Sues sisters.

I went to the front door and her sisters they greeted me with hugs, Peggy, Ethel and Peggy's daughter Rose, along with her sons, Bob and James and son in law Roger. They came in and walked around and said they would take everything. They even brought boxes with them. They lived about eighty miles away and Ethel had a second hand store and knew that when her sister did buy something it was quality. And hour and a half had passed and there wasn't anything left, all the cabinets had been cleaned out, even the garage, they took the fridge from the basement. The only appliances were in the kitchen. It was like a tornado had entered the house, I was happy they could use it. Peggy and Ethel asked what I was going to do with my life and I said that I had met someone and was going to start over. They wished me well and hugged me and thanked me for thinking of them, and then they departed. I called the pod container people and arraigned for a pick up the next day. They said I didn't have to be there, they would text and send an e-mail to verify the pickup. I checked the house and closed the windows and turned the climate control down and locked up. At least the curtains and blinds were still in place, so the house wouldn't look abandoned. I locked up and left.

I headed to the grocery store and followed the list Renee had given me, and added some cat food to it before I left the store and returned to my new home with Renee. When I arrived took everything to the kitchen, and unpacked the bags. Renee was in the laundry room, which was in the apartment and made things very convenient. Pits and Patter seemed to have adapted well. Renee said Pits liked following her around and when she had laid down, he was right there the whole time. I said he loves you, and that is good, and told her I was really surprised at how well they took to her. Said she was also surprised knowing cats acted funny sometimes. She used to have a cat but he passed away. I told her they sensed that, and was why they took to her. She looked at what I had brought home and started to prepare a meal for us. Told me to go and change, relax, and take a nap. I did just that, put my shorts on and laid in the second bed room and was joined by Patter, and soon I was asleep. I woke up a couple hours later to the smell of something smelling very good, used the bathroom, washed my hands and face and went to the kitchen and Renee was setting the table. She went and fixed the cats bowls, and asked me if I wanted some wine with dinner, and asked me to open the bottle in the fridge, I did and she began to fix our plates as I poured the wine, then she lite some candles and we sat down to eat.

It was one of the best dinners I had eaten in a very long time, you could taste the love. When I finished I told Renee so. Said it was just for me, the man in her life. It was the most wonderful meal I had eaten in a long time. I washed the dishes and placed them in the dish rack. When I finished, Renee took me by the hand and we sat on the couch. We sat together and I placed my arm around her and we relaxed and looked at some television until the news came on. She asked what I was going to do tomorrow. I told her we would go for a ride somewhere new and different. She lay down with her back in my lap and I placed a small pillow under her head, and we looked at each other as I felt her face and saw a loving and now very happy person, and I felt the same. After a while we left and made love before we showered together and went to bed, happy to be in each other's life. We hugged and kissed and sleep very well.

Nine

The following week everything went as planned. The pod was in storage; the painter had come and painted the whole house white inside. I had the carpets cleaned and a cleaning service came and cleaned the bathrooms and kitchen really well. Tommy listed the house on the RELS. Renee and I started to have a routine around the house, and said she liked it. It didn't remain on the market long and sold for the listed price.

We went several days a week to the different suburban neighborhoods looking and eventually we had narrowed it down to three areas, and that's when we went and started looking more closely at the actual listing. We also looked when we were at home. Several months had passed when we narrowed it down to five houses we liked. Yes we liked, because I asked Renee for her hand in marriage. I thought she would never stop crying, she eventually did and we were married before we found our new home. It was a simple ceremony at the court house. That was one of the happiest days in my life, I wouldn't be alone any longer and neither would she, we had each other.

When we did find the house, it had what I or rather we wanted, a very large bed room, which had originally been two out of four, with a very large bathroom, with a walk-in shower, tub, bidet, toilet, twin sinks and space for linen. The other two bedrooms shared a bathroom and were on the second floor also. There was a balcony off the master bedroom. The ground floor wasn't really on the ground, the elevation was three feet above ground, with a very large living room, dining room, library-study, kitchen and a full bath, the laundry room was ample in size with twin washers and dryers. The front entrance had a beautiful staircase to the upstairs, and there was even an elevator to all the levels. There was even a lovely staircase to the lower level or basement. It was equipped with a very large wet bar, pool table, full bathroom, and sauna. Was modern and only four years old and I had a backup generator installed. Pits and Patter couldn't decide where they wanted to be, and explored every corner of their new home. Renee and I bought a new car and a pickup. The garage was large, had space for four cars and I installed myself a wood and metal working shop. I used one bed room for our painting, sewing and as a hobby room; it had plenty of light with a porch and floor to ceiling windows. We had a full living room suite in our bed room and a king size bed suite. We weren't cramped by any means, and enjoyed decorating our new home. We even hired a house keeper to come once a week.

We traveled around the world, and when we returned, we were busy around the house and even became involved in some community activities. We loved one another and lived a beautiful life together, one that we both at one time would have never imagined possible. You know life is wonderful, because you never know what's in store for you. I had a person ask me one time would I like to be able to see into the future, and I replied no, and then they asked why. I said I would rather it be a surprise. It's the most wonderful thing to find a love you can cherish, and I had found that with Renee. Hope you do to:

The End

Three Short Stories

Calvin L Himel   10/20/20198

Other Stories from the Author

Location of Love
Four Girls plus One
Submissive Widow
The Story of Master Caesar

Three Short Stories
ISBN: 978-0-578-56641-2
Copyright: 2019

By C.L.Himel
10/20/2019

As I sit here looking out from my porch, I see the world as being full of wonderful people. I am going to tell you some stories about some real people, some of whom I have known, and maybe you even know. Some of these people are quite unique and will make you wonder, this could have been me, or it could have even been you. And then again, you may happen to know some of the characters mentioned, and just didn't know you really knew them.

Special People

It starts early one morning when Harvey Thrugburg, who was in his late teens, almost twenty, decided he was tired of fighting the overwhelming feeling that he had, that inside he was a woman. Harv, as he was known to his friends and family always seemed a little strange to them. He would dress secretly in women clothes and admire himself in the mirror. He was beautiful for a boy, and was only going to be hindered by time. That time it would take for him to come to grips with himself as to who he felt he really was, and how he would become comfortable with himself as a person of his own making. That would all change very soon little did he know. As a matter of fact, he was downright beautiful. He had since child hood, mastered his feelings and learned how to disguise how he felt from others.

He disliked his name, and was picked on in school in his early life, because of his feminine looks and smooth skin. He came from a family of mixed parentage. His father was part Irish, Italian, and Spanish. He was a very handsome man and was meticulous with his dress and appearance. He was one of the most handsome men in their town and his good looks helped him to become very popular, it also helped him hold a seat on the town council when he ran for public office. He owned a successful real-estate business and several low maintenance storage warehouses & strip malls. It didn't make them rich, but they didn't lack for very much either. His mother was a very beautiful woman; she had Indian, Spanish, African and English blood lines, with a beautiful brown completion and dark wavy hair, with an hour glass figure, and smooth flawless skin. She was a stay at home house wife most of the time when she wasn't helping her husband at his office. This combination gave Harvey his good but very feminine looks.

His parents did not tell Harv that he was born a hermaphrodite until later in life. I guess all families have a little secret. Mr. Thrugburg loved his wife Maria, and they both loved to party and dance. They loved Harvey very much being their only child, but knew Harvey was undecided as to what he wanted to be. Harvey at a young age played with boys and girls toys. One Christmas when the three of them were in the toy section they were a caught off guard when Harvey cried because he wanted a doll. But then they remembered what the doctor at birth had told them about their special child that the he or she would surface and they should be prepared as the child's personality developed. They purchased the doll and Harvey was happy. They were aware of the child's feeling most of the time, but many times they weren't fully aware of the mental implications due to the physical nature of the child.

In his early teens his mother sat him down and explained what made him different, and the reason why he might have a tendency to feel feminine at times. Harvey then began to better understand his own feelings. His mother also explained there was nothing to feel ashamed about that he could be male one day and female the next or maybe one day he would rather be more comfortable being a female and also told him that time would tell and that it would be up to him to decide and that she and his father understood he was different. She also made him aware that his body might change and that would help him determine who he would want to be. But most of all they loved him or her no matter what. She explained that she had researched the subject and that any decision he came to make would be his own and they would always support whatever decision he made because they loved him, and they only treated him like a boy because of his having a penis. Harvey went through grammar, middle & high schools as a boy, in appearance and in his school endeavors. Harvey was aware that he was different after his science studies in high school. His study of anatomy informed him of his being in that small percentage of special people, though he never revealed his being special to anyone.

Soon after graduation from high school he was working at a local restaurant, as a bus boy to earn some money before he returned to school in the fall. It was there that he met a young woman his age named Melisa. She really liked Harvey and they got along very well and they felt comfortable around one another. Melisa was very beautiful, and Harvey loved the way she spoke to him, and looked at him. Melisa was very shy like Harvey and they soon became very good friends. One evening after work Melisa asked Harvey if he would walk her home, they both lived nearby and not very far from the restaurant. Harvey agreed to walk Melisa home, and as they walked home Melisa was curious why Harvey did not have a girlfriend and asked Harvey just as he was wondering the same thing about her and why she didn't have any boyfriends. He explained that he had spent so much time studying to earn a scholarship that he really had not spent any time socializing or getting to know too many of the people he went to school with. Harvey had earned a scholarship for the local college in their area; and was going to major in art and business, and figured that explanation would allow him to keep hidden his true reason why he hadn't any friends, even from her. Melisa who had graduated from a private all-girls school that same spring, was going to attend the same school in the fall also; her major was going to be arts and science. Melisa said her parents were really liberal, and they were a happy family. Her parents, Sue and Bob were professionals, her dad was a dentist and her mom was a supervisor on her job at an insurance company, and also a member of the town library board. Melisa asked Harvey if he would like to stay for dinner, and meet her parents one evening after work. He said yes, why not and stayed to meet them. They discussed Melissa's and his going to college in the fall and had a delightful time. After dinner he and Melisa sat on the porch and talked for a while, before he left for home.

The following day at work, Harvey asked Melisa if she would come to his home and meet his parents, she immediately, said yes. They had a wonderful meal, and Harvey's parents were very happy that he had made a friend. Harvey had so few friends as he grew up; they were worried he might be introverted and uneasy about his physical appearance. Afterwards Harvey walked her home. The following day at work the two of them decided to go out on their day off. They planned to go see the latest movie at a theater that was known for showing artsy themed movies. They purchased their tickets and sat in the back rows in the center and Melissa reached for and held his hand often through most of the movie.

After the show they discussed there likes and dislikes, and Melisa who was keen to see that her friend was special, moved the subject to sex. Harvey senced where the conversation was headed and decided to be truthful with her, he valued their friendship and she was the first person outside of his parents he had spent any time with. He explained that he was very different, even though Harvey had taken a sex education course in school, he had not really comprehended what a special person he was until the day his mom sat him down and explained how different he was and what other changes might occur to him as he/she grew older. His chess had remained flat through school and he had no hair on his face or anywhere else on his body like many men. But recently he noticed he was starting to develop breast and his voice was changing and becoming more feminine. Not being sure if he should tell Melisa just how different he was, he decided to take a chance and confide in her anyway. She had noticed his many female peculiarities. He decided to tell her the real facts; he didn't want to hide from her any longer, for he really liked her. After he explained to her, about himself, she placed both her hands on his face and kissed him. He had never been kissed that way before. He felt amazed by her actions, and then she began to explain, that she too was different.

She was all female but had an overly large clitoris that could be considered a small penis and that made her feel like she was abnormal. She was also a virgin, like Harvey and had not had sex with another person; but said she masturbated and had busted her own cherry. She didn't care for a lot of the boys that she had met, but felt very attracted to Harvey. They continued to talk and decided to plan a coming out party. Harvey explained how he felt more and more like a girl sometimes and since working at the restaurant his breast were starting to get larger, and the nipples were starting to tingle. He had always masturbated since his early teens and being aware that he had a penis, but no testes and below that a vagina. When he masturbated, could be stimulated by both. She told him about how she stimulated herself, and they continued to confide in each other with a confidence that few couples do. They had never discussed this before with anyone, until now and both felt they would never find anyone else that they could trust and feel comfortable with.

A short time after their discussions about themselves, Harvey bought a used van from his uncle George who was a local car dealer for a real great price. Now he and Melissa didn't have to walk and decided to plan on spending a weekend together. They explained to their parents they were going to spend the weekend at a lodge camping with a group of pre-college students from their old high school. Their parents were happy that their introverted children were going out into the world, and happy they seemed to have found a trusting friend to be with, and besides they were both nineteen.

They decided to get a hotel room in the same town they lived in and had enough money to cover all their expenses and go shopping. Harvey and Melisa left that Saturday morning with the blessings of both sets of parents and were on their way. Melisa wanted to go to the forest preserves where some of their former friends from school were camping, and that way they could see them before setting out on their adventure into their new and very intimate and personal world together. Melisa had brought her makeup case and her hi heels, and several really nice dresses. She had packed all her stuff in her suit case and back pack while her parents were away at work. They drove around town catching the sights and sounds of their small but very vibrant city.

The two of them had made nineteen almost a year earlier and were looking forward to their twentieth birthdays soon. Their parents treated them both as adults. After a lunch at a fast food restaurant, they decided to check-in to their hotel room. They did the check in together as brother and sister. Their room was on the second floor of a two story motel, and after check in drove around to the entrance nearest their room location. They unloaded their bags and brought them up to their room. They both were filled with excitement and a little apprehension, for this was going to be Harvey's and Melisa's coming out party. They both could not wait to get their hands on the other, their passion growing with every waiting moment. After entering the room they stood and looked at each other and then embraced, kissing as they put their arms around each other and slowly began to remove each other clothing, their breathing getting short and more ragged, as their excitement grew. Soon they were both naked, standing and looking at one another. Melisa was a real beauty, her breast, was firm and much larger than Harvey's, but not too large, she was really shapely and in proportion, standing about five-six, smooth olive colored unblemished skin, brown eyes & hair down to her shoulders. Harvey stood transfixed, for he had never been with a nude girl before, let alone with one so beautiful and standing before him. He had an erection, his penis was standing at attention even though his appearance was more girl like than boy, and Melisa really noticed how feminine he was with his petite feet, hands and also his figure, his nipples were hard and erect, and his beautiful face really came through since he had not cut his hair in over a year and was almost as long as hers. A lot of boys were wearing their hair long so it wasn't unusual to see men with long hair. His lips were sensuous, his lashes long and his skin was very smooth.

They approached each other and began to caress one another. Neither had spoken a word since putting their bags in the room and locking the door. Melisa pulled Harvey to the bed and they both lay down looking at each other as they felt on one another. Harvey finally spoke and said he had never been with a girl before, and especially a naked one. Melisa said she had never been with a boy, and especially a naked one. She touched his penis and felt it throbbing in her hand; she slowly moved her hand lower and felt the opening that was his vagina. He moaned and the feelings were total ecstasy, he had never had that feeling before, being touched by someone other than himself. He felt her breast as he slowly move his hand between her legs and felt the moisture as she opened them more so he could put a finger inside of her. He looked and felt her large erect clit, and the way she moaned as he touched her. They felt each other, kissed as the heat between them grew until they both had an orgasm together just from touching and feeling each other. They lay their together holding each other, as their breathing slowly returned to normal.

Harv got up off the bed and retrieved his duffel bag and removed a latex dildo about twelve inches long, and some antiseptic jelly. He came over to the bed and showed Melisa the dildo. She knew what it was for and was ready for their sexual adventure, he lubed it up and laid on his back and she took it from him as she placed her head near his erect penis. She took the dildo as she caressed his hardness. Then she moved her hot open mouth to his penis and began to lick it, then she put it in her mouth as she slowly moved her head up and down, and moved her tongue all around it and then she slowly placed the dildo into his wet vagina, he moved his body up & down and shortly afterwards had the biggest climax of his life, as she took his full load down her throat. After a few minutes he sat up and looked up at her and they kiss as his cum dripped from her sweet lips. Harvey put her on her back and began kissing her from her head and slowly licked her neck and down to her very erect nipples, to her navel and finally ending at her shaven and swollen pulsating pussy, licking her pussy lips as he spread her thighs wide and licked and sucked her massive oversized clit. He licked the inside of her vulva and then licked her clit, and then he sucked it like the short thick and wide looking penis it was while he gently slid the dildo gently inside of her. It wasn't long before she too had a massive climax that rocked her body that seemed un-stoppable. She laid there breathless for it seems eternity, before Harvey climbed on top of her and placed his rock hard penis in her throbbing pussy, and at first slowly pushed it inside of her. The pleasure was unlike anything she had experienced, and for Harvey had never been inside a woman and the warmth from her pussy was the best feeling he had ever experienced, then after several minutes Melissa asked him to stick himself in her anus, Harvey pulled out and grabbed both her legs and raised them and placed his hard penis in her anus which was wide open, and as he inserted himself almost all the way in, he climaxed again. They lay next to each other as they regained their breath before picking each other up as they kissed before heading to the bathroom to shower.

They bathed each other and feeling each other more as they had more sex before cleaning their toy as they kissed and fondled each other as they showered. They dried each other off and then went to the bed as Melisa removed a bottle of body oil from her bag and brought it over to the bed where she began to rub Harvey with-it and he took some and began to oil her. Since they were both exhausted and relieved and were really hungry. They decided to go to dinner, at the restaurant attached to the motel, which was on the classy side. It was time for Harvey to come out. Harvey was going to dress like the woman he felt he was. He had brought his female clothing and other items, it wasn't much, but he had accumulated makeup, lipstick, pantyhose over the past years and especially over the last year as he was really starting to feel his feminine side come out more. Melisa was real excited about being with her best boy-girl friend. They used the iron that was in the room to touch up their clothes. She had brought several of her best shoes and they both wore the same size shoe. Her and his shoe sizes were the same, for they were only an inch difference in height, and only five pounds different in weight. She had brought several dresses, and he had brought the only two he had. They ironed their clothes, before they put on some clear nail polish, did their hands and toes, they didn't want to be too flashy and draw any undue attention. They dressed and Melissa helped Harvey dress, his shape was real feminine, but had been hidden in baggy clothes all this time.

They went into the bath room together to put on their make-up. Melisa helped Harvey lightly apply his and showed him some tricks in its application, for they were young and had taken care of their skin very well for young people and their acne had long since passed. Harvey was now to become Harriot. She was beautiful as they took pictures, and Harriot had no problems walking in the high heels, and she wore a pair of Melisa shoes, some really cute open toe shoes, some clip-on earrings, necklace and perfume. They were a most stunning pair together. They left their room and went downstairs to the restaurant, No one would know that Harriot was a hermaphrodite, she was cute and very graceful, so much so that after they were seated in a corner booth, that Melisa said to her that she was really super beautiful as a woman, and now she knew what had attracted her so much. They were approached by their waitress for their order, since they had worked up such an appetite, they decided on dinner. They both ordered similar meals, a fish entrée with baked potato & a salad, and soft drinks. Their waitress complemented them on how well they were dressed, as she left to place their orders.

Harriett told Melisa that the waitress was a girl that he had gone to high school with and that she had no clue as to who he was. When there food arrived they ate slowly and took in the atmosphere of the restaurant with it chandeliers, deep cushioned booths and warm decor. They declined desert, paid and left. After they finished they took a walk and window shopped at some of the nearby stores before heading back to their room. Before returning to their room they grabbed some pop & snacks from the vending machines in the motel. They went to the room and took the ice bucket and then ducked out for the ice machine, after returning, they took glamour photos of one another. They had a filling meal and turned on the television and dialed in some sex movies as they proceeded to make some drinks. Harriett had brought a bottle of rum from home, his father always had plenty, and people were always giving them liquor as gifts around the holidays, more than they cared for since his dad had a favorite, and he just let the others sit and accumulate for guest. Harriett fixed her and Melissa some rum and cokes, as Melissa began to undress.

They sipped their drinks as Harriett began to undress, and soon were fondling each other again as they looked at some porn movies on the television which caused them to become more aroused. They caressed each other with great passion, with both being highly aroused, and soon Harriett was sucking Melissa's toes, and shortly after they had assumed the 69 position as Melissa took him in her mouth as she fingered his pussy and ass, and he sucked on her throbbing clit and put his fingers deep in her pussy and anus. Both were really enjoying each other, soon both were climaxing at the same time and it lasted for several long minutes before they released each other exhausted. Wow said Melissa as she sat up with difficulty, drained, and very satisfied. Harriett laid there with labored breathing, as Melissa slowly climbed on top of him and they began to kiss with their juices mingling. They slowly got up and took another shower together, and fondled each other as they bathed. Melissa took her morning after pill. She suggested that Harriet take one also for she had read of a hermaphrodite getting pregnant. So he took it without hesitation. After showering and returning to the room, they finished their drinks and got in bed together, snuggling up before falling fast asleep.

Sunday morning came as they woke up just in time to get dressed for breakfast. Harvey said he was going as Harriett, since it was much easier to dress and was becoming more and more comfortable being Harriett and it was easier to just slip on a dress and panties. He was good at tucking his much relaxed circumcised penis in panties between his legs, it didn't even show, not even a little bit, Melisa was so amassed at that. They casually went to breakfast, hungry as hell; the motel had a full buffet and they ate their fill before returning to their room. Since it was Sunday, they were going to have to check out before noon, so they decided to pack and then spend the rest of the day at the mall. But before they would have to go they had a couple hours and decided to make the best of it, they undressed and lay in the bed feeling each other and having more sex and showers before having to go.

They finally checked out at the last minute, packed up the van, and headed for the mall. Harvey was still dressed as Harriett, and they discussed what he was going to do when they headed home. Harvey said he was going to tell his parents, they understood his predicament, and whatever decisions, or conclusions he came to was the right thing for him-her to do. And especially since so many people were coming out of the closet, and then there were the transgender people who were also being seen and heard. Melissa agreed with him and asked if he wanted her to be there when he presented himself to his parents, said he was undecided at that time and felt that he should do it on his-her own.

Melissa told him that she loved him and wanted a steady relationship and he agreed with her. He was more self-confident than ever before and he felt their relationship had a positive effect on him. They arrived at the mall and did some shopping. Harriett bought some new dresses and several pairs of shoes, and decided to get her ears pierced, which she did. Melissa bought some shoes and jewelry while Harriett was getting her ears pierced. Now she felt more complete. It was getting late and it was time to head home. Soon they headed to the parking lot, and on their way passed some boys who whistled as they passed, Harriett had more a since of self-confidence at being the woman he-she had always wanted to be, now that everyone who saw him, saw as a woman now. They arrived at Melissa's home first and they kissed and Melissa said she would call him later to see how it went with his parents. She told him how much of a great time she had, as she walked toward her front door and waved good bye for now. Harvey got home and found his parents were not at home, he thought this would be a good time to clean up and get ready for them to return. He unpacked and put his cloths away and decided he would be Harriett when they arrived home. About two hours later they returned. Harriett was dressed in a black dress above the knees, with some cleavage showing, hi heels, necklace, and his curly hair up in a bun. She was a stunning beauty.

His parents entered the house and called out his name since they had seen his van in the driveway. Harvey answered and then went into the living room where both were having a conversation. His mother was sitting on the sofa and his dad was standing near the front door when Harriett entered the room and said hello: they both looked at her and his father almost fainted, as his mother gasp, he told them that after all the years feeling the way he did, he was tired of hiding his feelings. His mother stood and walked to where she was standing and with tears of joy hugged him and told him she loved him, and that whatever he decided was ok with her. His dad came over and hugged him also giving his approval, for he had lost his son only to have gained the most beautiful daughter a father could have. They stood there hugging and crying tears of joy, since they knew that this might happen one day. He told them his name was Harriett now, and that he felt more secure in his being a woman. His parents were so elated that dad suggested they go out for dinner and celebrate.

At dinner she asked her father about being an intern in his business in the fall while she attended college, he was more than happy, and glad she had asked. This was turning out to be a very happy occasion for everyone. They discussed changing his/her name legally, and other things, such as when she attended college her living at home, and helping her dad. A lot was happening, and all for the better. After dinner they happily went home and as soon as they were their her father suggested that they have a drink to celebrate, and so they sat down and Harriett had herself a rum & coke, while her father had his aged bourbon and mom her scotch. After all that had happened, they all headed to bed, her father hugged her tight and told her he loved her no matter what, and was glad she had found herself. Mother hugged and kissed her and said she knew one day she would find herself.

Harriett just had to call Melissa and tell her of the wonderful evening that had just occurred. Melisa said she really wanted to see her the next day; she missed her already after their weekend together. The next day before noon Melissa came over and they talked, she asked what she was going to do about her job at the restaurant, Harriett said she was going in as Harvey and resign, and then the last of his life as Harvey would be taken care of, and would put it to a close. He stated that her father said that after he had taken care of the loose ends of being Harvey she could come and work for him part time and start learning the real-estate business.

Harvey said that her mother wanted to go shopping and help her change her wardrobe. Melissa said she wanted to go with Harriett and her mother. Melissa and Harriett were in love with one another. Melissa said she wanted to give Harriett space to be herself and would not try to be too possessive. Harriett said she needed the support of Melissa and her love for her was what helped him make the transition to female. They both agreed to be loving friends and support each other and not to be possessive, with that they kissed their passionate kiss.

Harriett's mother & father were away for the day, so they went to her room where they had each other and their passions erupted. Melissa disrobed and got on her knees and pulled Harriett to her as she raised her skirt and pulled her panties down and took Harriett in her mouth causing her penis to rise to the occasion. She caressed her throbbing penis with her tongue & mouth, as Harriett removed her cloths and was naked, she grabbed Melisa and pulled her to her feet and led her to the bed, Harriett bent Melissa over on her knees with her ass up and got behind her and slid her penis into her now

95

hot and throbbing pussy, slowly at first, sliding in and out then harder as Melissa moaned with passion as Harriet slid her finger into her anus, causing it to relax and open, just as Melissa started to climax, Harriett pulled her dick out of Melissa's throbbing wet pussy and stuck it up her open anus, as Melissa orgasm intensified, she reached around and rubbed her clit, bringing her to a super climax as her penis went deeper into her anus, soon she was shooting hot sperm up Melissa's anus as she moaned with pleasure. Harriett rolled Melissa over on her back, spread her legs and pulled her to the end of the bed, grabbed her ankles, spread her legs as she got on her knees and ate her pussy sending Melissa over the edge again with a passion she could never have imagined. Then she climbed on top of her and they kissed passionately.

After kissing and feeling each other they went and took a quick shower, before her parents got home. They decided that he would go to the restaurant as Harvey and resign. Harvey was going to make this his last appearance as a male. Melissa was going to resign also because she could not be their without her best friend. So they climbed into the van, Harriett was dressed as Harvey, and off they went. When they arrived at the restaurant they found the owner and resigned together. Since it was close to school starting the owned understood and paid them their wages and wished them well.

They left and decided to go to the park and talk. This was going to be one of the last times for Harvey to be seen as a male, so he wanted to make the best of it. Melissa and him parked and got out and walked one of the many walking paths as they held hands and talked and spoke of how wonderful it was that they had met, what they thought the future held for them, and what they would do tomorrow, for they just could not keep their hands off each other. They promised that they would keep their relationship exclusive and they both agreed that since they had difficulties with other people the best thing for them was to cherish each other and that way be safe from STDs. They talked about whether or not once they started school; they should get an apartment together, but in order to save money and since their parents were supportive that might not be such a good idea. They decide that the better choice would be to live at home, save their money as they planned their future. They headed back to the van, and Harvey took Melissa home. Melissa asked if she would like to come in, but she declined and said she would like to be Harriett the next time he saw her parents, she agreed, kissed him for the last time, and said she would see her tomorrow.

The next day Harriette came over to Melissa's home and since it was early Saturday morning, both her parents were home, at first they did not realize Harriett was the former Harvey, she sat down and explained what her life was like and how she was different. How Melissa had been a part of her coming out. They were amazed, but since they knew their daughter was also special, it was not difficult for them to understand. They were happy for the both of them, and glad they had found one another. Melissa's parents suggested that they go to lunch together, and asked Harriette if her parents were home and available and they could all go together. Harriett called home and handed the phone to Melissa's dad. After a few minutes he hung up and announced that Harriett's parents had instead suggested they go to dinner later that day, and he agreed.

They would all meet at a nearby restaurant that was upscale and have dinner at six and Mr. Thrugburg would call ahead and make the reservations. Melissa and Harriette were elated. Harriette started to cry for she felt that she had really been accepted in her new role as a woman as Melissa came and hugged her, and they held each other tight. Harriett thanked Melissa's parents for being so understanding, and said she had to go home and prepare for the evening ahead. Melissa walked her to the door, kissed her and told her she loved her, and would see her later.

That evening everyone was dressed, the fathers wore suits and their mothers were beautiful, wearing their jewelry, high heels and looking there finest. Melissa and Harriett were exceptionally dressed; they wore dresses above the knee showing there exceptionally beautiful figures, open toe high heels and earrings and jewelry, their nails and toes were polished. Their parents knew one another from their business relationships and being on different boards within the community. When they entered, they were promptly seated in one large booth shaped like a half moon. Melissa and Harriette were seated together in the center with their parents flanking them on both sides. Melissa and Harriette held hands under the table. It was a joyous occasion and after the orders for the food was placed, Harriett's father, ordered a bottle of Champaign.

Everyone toasted the occasion and Harriette thanked everyone for their acceptance of her decision, and thanked her new best friend for helping her overcome her fears of being herself. It was a joyous occasion and Harriette said it was the best day of her life. Everyone enjoyed their food and had dessert afterwards. The party departed and decided they would get-together more often.

Several months passed and all was working out well for Harriett and Melissa. By the time they had graduated from junior college, they had opened a clothing store and were very successful and living together happily. They married and it was the only time Harriette wore a man's suit, she said it just appeared more natural, and they lived happily ever after.

The End

Alien Love Encounter

Alien Love Encounter

It started out as just a cross country trip to see some of the faraway places in the United States. I had decided to take a couple months away from the everyday business of going to work in the antique shop and specialty stores I owned and had a partnership interest in. It was early spring and the weather was pleasant for traveling especially after the winter holidays. I had left my suburban Chicago home and decide I wanted to see more of the western states than I had before when I was in the military and when my now deceased father lived in Orange County California. I traveled the interstate road system southwest from Chicago stopping in St. Louis after staying in Springfield Illinois for a day. I headed through Missouri to Oklahoma and Texas stopping along the way staying a day or two in various locations and taking in the flavor of the different locations. Traveled through New Mexico, Arizona to California, and I didn't realize how large California was until I started to transverse the state east to west. I knew it was going to be a long drive north and traveled the famous pacific coast highway and took in the scenery. Oregon and Washington State were also beautiful to travel through especially the forest and smelling that humid primal forest air. After reaching Seattle decided to head back east but decided going through Idaho and Montana instead of going back the way I came through the southwestern states of New Mexico, Texas and Arizona. I wanted to always see Montana; it seemed so far away but yet so close to Illinois where I live. It was one of the least populated states as far as I knew. First let me introduce myself, and tell you a little about myself. My name is Calzone Howard, thirty six years old. I am of mixed blood and have the uncanny ability to blend in with a lot of different groups of people. Both my parents were from the southern united states, on my mother's side of the family there was a mixture of native American, African and Irish, with my great, great, great grandfather coming to the state of Mississippi before it was even a state in 1820, there the family blood line mixed with Indian and Africans to provide me with a very rich heritage. On my father's side of the family came from Louisiana, with French, Africa, Spanish and German blood lines. The family spoke creole French, and I had taken German in grammar school and some Spanish in high school, which gave me some advantage when I was in the United States army. I served during the Vietnam era and went to Vietnam and Germany. Fortunately, I almost went around the world and have come to appreciate our way of life in these United States. I am always on the lookout for unusual items, and had left my first assistant Marie Hopeland in charge of my business and didn't have any worries since she had a stake in the operation. She manages the day to day operations while I scout out various estate sales and travel throughout the country looking for and finding unusual items. I am more of a silent partner in the specialty stores than an active one. One store is an antique store that we have together and carry many usually and odd things because we have some highly eccentric clients.

Well anyway I was enjoying the drive seeing the sights, hills and valleys and the ever changing terrain of the United States. The American landscape is just beautiful when you consider that we have a sample of every terrain on the planet right here, from deserts and forest to tropical and just flat land, like the Great Plains. I had just left the hamlet of Hinsdale Montana heading east on state highway 2 taking in the vast landscape. I had been driving just about all day and had just topped off my gas tank, the sun was starting to set and I had hoped to make it to Glasgow Montana before night fall, but that wasn't going to happen too soon and really wasn't on a schedule so I pulled over and took a break, taking a pee by the side of the road and stretching my legs, taking out a cigarette and having a smoke. One thing for sure about Montana is that you can drive for hours and never see another car, truck or anything else which didn't bother me; I kind of liked it in a sense as it gives you time to get in touch with yourself.

After driving for several hours as dust approached I noticed a light in the distance sky and didn't think much about it and figured it was an aircraft way off in the distance. The sky is so beautiful in Montana, as I was thinking it would be a nice quiet place to settle down and have real peace of mind away from the hustle and bustle of city life. I had stopped and had just finished smoking my cigarette, returning and getting back in my crew cab pickup after having pulled off the road for a short time to stretch my legs before continuing on my journey east. When I noticed the light in the sky becoming larger and was coming closer and fast before I realized it might be a plane getting ready to land. I didn't see the red and green lights associated with an aircraft. As it came closer, it slowed down and looked like it was landing and figure it could be an aircraft but then it just headed toward the ground and disappeared. I figured it landed nearby but then several minutes later, like ten or fifteen a bright light just flashed from the area where the light had disappeared. I figured it was at least five miles away or so. Oh well, I figured this is Montana and wasn't familiar with the surrounding country side and there could be and air strip nearby and with the state being so vast it was possible quite a few people had airplanes, like in Alaska with its many bush pilots. I continued driving and the next thing I know some fifteen minutes later a military fighter plane passes low overhead and continued on before it circled around where the light had emanated from and then returned in the direction it had come from.

I continued driving and after several miles, maybe four or five I saw up ahead what looked like a person standing by the side of the road, they had their hand out trying to get me to stop. I wasn't keen on picking up hitchhikers because you never know who it might be, but then the strangest thing happened, I heard a voice in my head. It said please help me, and as I started slowing down, I could see as I got closer that it appeared to be a woman, she was very dark skinned and was dressed in a skin tight suit, almost semi metallic in appearance as I slowed to a stop. I'm thinking what is she doing out here since I hadn't seen any black folks since leaving Washington state. She had a very beautiful face, her skin was very dark, and she had very keen features, and was about a little more than five feet tall. I asked her where she was headed. She didn't speak with her mouth but with her mind, which I heard very clearly, she asked me to please take her with me. I said ok and opened the passenger door for her, but before she got in she retrieved a metallic looking round bag from the side of the road and placed it in her lap after she got in. I told her to buckle up, and she understood as I started to pull off and continued to drive and asked what is a pretty black woman doing out here in the middle of nowhere. She spoke to me telepathically as I continued to drive, said I had nothing to fear, she had read my thoughts and knew I was an open minded person about a lot of things. She would be able to speak verbally shortly after her body became more adjusted to our atmosphere. Said that she had been traveling, based on our time count about fifty years at a thousand times the speed of light, she was the last of her kind and had traveled from another galaxy. I said really, you are from another world, ok but that kind of sounds fantastic. I said aliens are supposed to be small and green, and then I began to laugh which kind of caught her guard and said she didn't understand. She said that a great disturbance had come to her part of the universe and the elders had chosen hundreds of fertile young women and men to travel to unknown parts of the universe, most went as couples and when the available males ran out the older single women were sent alone to galaxies much further away and she was one of those. She had passed through several galaxies before her ship had chosen this solar system and this particular planet and this is where she landed. Before landing, her ship had circled this planet more than a dozen times, as her ship slowed down it began intercepting communications from all over the planet and placed the information in the small device she had with her that would soon allow her to communicate directly with me after her body had adjusted to our atmosphere. I asked her why here in Montana? She replied because there were fewer people here than anywhere else and her device had told her it was in one of the strongest nations on this world. That the probability of blending in would be much better here as I laughed, and thought about her color and where we were.

I said to her, well welcome to earth sweetheart. I didn't feel frightened by her presence and felt very comfortable with her. I didn't know why I didn't have any concerns about catching any disease or other adverse effects she might be having on me, and she didn't appear to be hostile. I said you need to put on some earth clothes, some earth people are hostile, and having dark skin wasn't always a plus and would explain later. Said that there had been a military aircraft that had circled where she had landed and they were sure to investigate the landing sight soon as they could find it. Said I had some extra clothes that she could slip over what she had on because dressed like she was could only be one of two things, she was a stripper or an alien. She thanked me and I soon pulled over at a deserted roadside break area, which was nothing more than a few picnic tables and some garbage cans. I reached in my bag and took them out, a pair of jeans and a long sleeve shirt out; I handed them to her, and went and had another smoke. She put them on over her clothes and they fit her slim figure with no trouble. I said to her I hope you destroyed you craft because the military and government would like to get hold of your technology and especially you for their experiments and your life would no longer be yours and whatever hope you had of survival would surely come to an end. She asked me why I wasn't frightened of her. Said I was more frightened of other humans than her. Joking I said there wasn't anything to be frightened of as long as she didn't want to eat me, which she didn't understand. Told her I knew we on this planet weren't the only people or beings in the vast reaches of the cosmos, and always hoped to see a vessel or being from another world. She said that her craft had self-destructed after it determined her destination had been reached and she was on her own as far as survival was concerned, and that some people might be hostile to her kind and the device she had with her was giving her information all the time. This planet was chosen because of the atmosphere being similar to her home planet and most of the life forms were very similar. That her device, something like a computer as we knew it but way more advanced was giving her inputs as I spoke to her, she had her hand on the top of the bag and a slight glow could be seen under her hand. We got back in the truck and I continued to drive and we finally reached Glasgow, I stopped and filled my gas tank. While filling my tank noticed a small military convoy headed in the direction we had just come from. I said there they go looking for you and your ship. As she sat in the truck she told me they wouldn't find anything much more than some burnt metal. I said metals not from here. I figured we should just lay low because they would never figure on a black alien landing on earth and had to laugh to myself as I thought black folks would probably want to leave earth if we had a chance.

Afterwards I went and registered and got us a room at the Stairway Lodge Motel. I was tired and had been up close to eighteen hours. We checked in as husband and wife. I pulled around to where our room was, and was glad there were only a few guests. Brought my bags inside, along with my new friend, as I finally got around to asking her if she had a name, she said her name was Lumia. I stopped speaking verbally and just communicated with my mind. She asked me to continue speaking out loud so she could better understand my language. She said the device had recorded various languages as it circled the planet and asked me which was the one I was speaking. I said with my mind it was called English. I asked what types of food do you eat, and do you drink water. Lumia replied that she drank water and the foods she observed that we ate were similar with her previous diet. I asked if she was a female like females here. I explained that we on earth had males and females. She said it was the same on her world and had observed from our communication, we were similar or the same. I asked her if they bathed, she replied yes. She took the clothes off I had given her and began to remove her suit and boot like shoes. She stood before me naked, and asked me if she looked like a human female and asked me to examine her. I was stunned by her beauty and her wanting me to look at her and not being afraid of me, as I stood stunned and looked at her. Then she spoke with her mouth and said, don't be afraid. I said great you can talk. She said yes, and told me she understood my language completely.

I looked at her beautiful body closely as she reached out and touched my hand. Her touch felt normal, I mean her body temperature was the same and her skin was very smooth and flawless. She had five fingers on both hands and five toes, her limbs were slender and the curves were all in the right place, her color was chocolate in appearance and very smooth, her hair was short and wavy, her breast were small and firm, with nipples that were large in diameter and long in length, her waist was small, and she had very round buttocks, and she must have read my mind, because then she laid on the bed and spread her legs wide open, her hairless vagina looked like any human females, then the lips opened and appeared as a perfect vertical mouth with small perfect lips and as if by reflex and a small penis looking clit appeared at the top, coming out about an inch as it grew wider, it extended itself almost two inches, before it retracted and the lips closed. She sat up. Lumia explained that from all her device had told her, she was compatible with humans, her physical appearance was the same, and she could consume the food we ate but her diet demanded more plant based foods.

I asked her if she wanted to bath in water. I explained that water was H2O; she stated that she understood the periodic table of elements and understood. Said she welcomed it. Lumia said I had been chosen by her device, it had informed her after scanning the communication frequencies and analyzing me from a distance that I wasn't hostile and had peaceful intentions. She had hid by the side of the road and her device had warned her of my approach, and had analyzed me more than a mile away, had told her I wasn't hostile and had an open mind when it came to unusual things or happenings. I spoke to her and she spoke back and called me friend. I said yes, but I had a name, and it was Calzone. Calzone she said verbally. Her English was very good. I asked about her language. She replied that it wasn't important any longer because she had no way to return and her planet didn't exist any longer that her device had informed her of such. I asked her if she was the only one to land on earth. She said her device had told her one other ship had followed her but crashed on a neighboring planet.

I said that I was going to bathe in some water or H20. She said that she would also. After I undressed, said she wanted to look at me. I stood as she came over and looked me up and down, asked me to lie in the bed and spread my legs open, I complied as she looked closely. She was satisfied with her observation and asked me to stand. Stated I looked like the males on her home world. We entered the bathroom, and I sat on the toilet and defecated, and said she understood the use and asked the name of the device. Said it was called a toilet or commode and had several other names. When I finished and used the toilet paper, she communicated that she understood how it functioned. I had brought my bottled water with me and she drank some, she coughed at first. Said it was sweet to her taste, and asked if all water tasted the same. I said no but this was plain water, H2O. Said she understood the periodic chart of elements. I turned the water on, and waited for it to warm up, and asked her to see if it was too hot for her. Lumia said it was to cool, I told her I would have to bath first because it could get a lot hotter than I could stand. I entered the shower and lathered up and rinsed off. When I stepped out and showed her the soap and said it was for cleaning the body and then showed her how to control the temperature, she stepped in and turned the temperature control up almost as far as it would go and she bathed herself and seemed to enjoy it as the bathroom filled with steam. Shortly she stepped out as I handed her a towel from the hotel, and she said it was very hard and scratchy. I went and took a towel from my bag and returned and handed it to her and she smiled, and said soft. Then standing there before me nude her body literally filled out before my eyes. Lumia's body expanded, her height increased by six inches, I was six feet two inches and now she stood almost six feet tall, her breast increased in size as well as her butt, thighs and feet. She was the tallest, most shapely woman I had ever seen. She saw the look on my face, and explained to me it was because of the time spent in space and coming out of a suspended state. Told me she had now reached full maturity and there was one other step she had to take to be able to adjust to her new planet. Told me she had to copulate with me for her genes to become immune to the diseases on this world.

Yes she replied to me telepathically, sex. She had read my mind and I wondered about my hidden thoughts. A sexual encounter was necessary for her complete transformation. Asked me to please have sex with her and it would also help me, because there would be a transfer of fluids and it would enhance my immune system also. She read my mind as far as four-play was concerned, and replied it was also part of the mating ritual. We climbed into bed, I retrieved a bottle of olive oil I carried with me and before I started to apply some to myself. Lumia took the bottle and smelled it, placed some on her finger and said Womp. I explained to her it was from a tree and was used for cooking, and lubrication and had many uses. Said I was going to put some on my body to keep, the skin moist and soft. Lumia said they had olive oil on her world. I asked her if I could apply some to her and she welcomed it and would do me. I oiled her and massaged her and felt the firmness of her beautiful body and the soft smoothness of her skin and how warm she felt, then she did the same to me and when we were finished she took me in her soft hands and I felt her, she felt just like a normal earth woman, she felt me and I just went into my love mode and forgot that she was from another world, and I kissed her and felt her all over and she had some wild moves and soon I was on top of her as I licked her ear and she guided me inside of her and I could feel her clit as it moved around and it became large and warm, then she rocked below me and she wrapped her arms around me and held me, as I felt my penis being massaged inside her vagina without me even moving and then I had this massive climax, unlike anything I had ever had before, of course it had been a couple weeks since I had last climaxed, and that was when I had last masturbated. She held me as I could feel her vagina just milking my penis. She released me and when I pulled out I was exhausted and rolled to the side of her. Lumia turned to face me and rolled me on my back and climbed on top of me, straddled me and placed her hands on both sides of my head, my eyes began to close and it was like I had entered a state of deep sleep. My mind was filled with stars and I was taken to a very beautiful place, I couldn't begin to describe it, then my mind began to fill with knowledge, it flashed past so quickly and then it came to a climax, and I entered a very deep state of sleep. When I awoke seven hours had passed, I felt more rested than ever before in life, if I thought about something, it seemed the answer was right there. I opened my eyes and Lumia was lying beside me, she had pulled the covers over both of us, and she was holding my hand. She spoke to me again telepathically, said that her body was adjusting and she would soon awaken. I just laid there as my mind started getting adjusted to my new thoughts and the new way of thinking and especially about the last twenty-four hours. About twenty minutes or so later her eyes opened and she sat up.

Lumia said all had gone very well, her body had taken me in and she had transferred to me the antibodies for a long and healthy life, along with new neural connections that would allow me to use my entire brain. I looked at her, and she sensed what was on my mind as we reached for one another, and kissed and she said we now were one. I looked at the clock, good thing I had booked the room for two days, sometimes on these trips I would just sleep for more than half a day. I felt energized, but was very hungry and it was early afternoon. I looked at my space lover; we were one. I thought and soon realized what that really meant. Lumia said I could speak to her without speaking verbally with my voice, and could just use my mind. I seemed to have the ability to read her thoughts as well, yes she replied and it would become more enhanced as time went on. I turned on the television and the local news was on and the authorities were investigating what they said was a plane crash about eighty miles away. I knew what that was, but she seemed unconcerned. Lumia said she needed nourishment, and I agreed with her.

Fortunate thing was, she could wear my clothes, I gave her a pair of socks to fill up the shoes, I wore a twelve and her feet were slightly smaller but in proportion to her size. My clothes were clean and gave her some underwear and a pair of jeans and a t-shirt, and they fit her well. We drove to the nearest restaurant and we went inside. At least we didn't draw any undue attention except for the fact they probably didn't see many dark skinned people around here. I thought to myself, plant based vegetables or a salad. When I asked her about eating animals, a protein based substance. She declined until there was a better selection. I said beans are plant based and are high in protein. I ordered for both of us, we ordered a bean soup, and a couple of chicken salads. Soon the food came and we ate. Telepathically she told me I was right after tasting the soup and I asked the waitress for some red pepper or cayenne. Lumia said peppers were one of the staples where she came from, and told her she would love my cooking. I asked her about fish, said yes they had fish as we called them, but baked them depending on the type and some were boiled and others fried. We finished eating and returned to the motel to get my stuff, and I asked Lumia if she wanted to shower again, she responded yes and she went and spent five minutes in the very warm shower. I went after and took one also. We dried off and stood looking at one another. She read my thoughts and said yes, but we needed to leave. We dressed and I turned in the key at the front desk and we headed out of town, and headed east.

I continued on route 2, east and then 25, to Wolf Point to 13 south, then route 2005 to Glendive and interstate 94. We stopped several times on the way home and I took Lumia to several big box stores along the way and bought her clothes that were for females, she commented on the clothing for her sex. Said at least there were many choices, but some seemed so primitive.

Two days after my encounter, we arrived at my suburban home outside of Chicago. Once we arrived, I said to her welcome to my humble abode. By now she had pretty much comprehended the entire English language, including slang. I showed her my library and said this is a tiny amount of the sum of human knowledge. Lumia said she understood, and said I would comprehend more. I showed her the computer and the internet. She placed her device next to the modem on my desk. It began to glow, then it flashed several colors as it did, Lumia explained it was exploring. I said you may not want to bring unwanted attention to us. She touched the device as it emitted a dull color and, she said that it hadn't accessed anything that would bring undue attention. The device had informed her that we were safe. She asked me to place my hand on it, since we were one she explained it needed my, she said we called it, vibe. I placed my hand on the device it was cool to the touch, it glowed blue, a shade so beautiful I was amazed. It communicated with me, and said I could remove my hand. Lumia told me that I would be able to receive information from the device. I asked her about power to the device and said it drew power from the atmosphere and was constantly charging itself.

I prepared a meal for us, I had some beans that I had prepared and they were frozen, and I fixed some rice with veggies and a salad with tomatoes and radishes and cucumbers. Every time I pulled out a veggie Lumia said something in her native language. I showed her some chicken and began to season a couple of breast after they had thawed and seasoned them before I prepared to bake them. When everything had finished cooking, I set the table and pulled a bottle of red wine from the fridge. I dished up the food and poured the wine into glasses. We sat down and began eating. She at first smelled all the food before she consumed it and said it was delicious. She asked for more, and of course I served it to her. When she finished said that she was fully satisfied now. I showed her the television and she said that other than using it as a learning tool to understand her new home we as a race were being manipulated by greedy people. I showed her a book to back up her assessment. She asked if you know, why it is this way, and handed her several more books which she read in a couple hours. Said now she understood, but it shouldn't be this way, I said I agreed with her that all the resources were being wasted, for just a few greedy people. That one day would soon come when mankind would face its greatest challenge, and that would be extinction.

We prepared to sleep, I showed her the bathroom, and she communicated to me that since we were now one there weren't any secrets between us. We use the facilities together and she said we could shower together also, her body had slowly adapted to earth more and more. She had seen that I was a minority, and based on her color she was also. I was thinking she would never be safe if it was known there were black aliens, and she answered yes as she read my thoughts. Lumia said it was more important that we copulate more, she said it was a natural pleasure no one could take from us. We finished cleaning ourselves and dried off. Said the towels here were the softest and felt good against her skin. We went to the bed room and I laid out a dry towel and told her I would oil her body, and said she looked forward to the placing of hands as she called it. I oiled her and she loved the way I felt her all over and especially when I felt her between her legs, it caused her to have spasms as she just reached out and flipped me on my back and began feeling me all over and I had to get her to use the oil and she poured it on me and then she rubbed it all over me, she was strong as she turned me over and rubbed me, I had a hard on that wouldn't quit and she sat on me as I laid on my back, then she laid on top of me with her arms at my side and looked me in my eyes, as she rocked slowly back and forth I saw her eyes glow and the stimulation I was feeling was enormous, unlike anything I had ever felt before, I reached up and felt her breast, and I felt the hard nipples and I squeezed them and a smile came to her face as they became larger and played with them, as the pleasure in me grew and I squeezed her nipples and as I climaxed she did also and let out a scream unlike anything I had ever heard in my life, then she laid on top of me panting very hard, soon it subsided. She rolled over on her side and she pulled me next to her and held me kissing me wildly for several long minutes. She telepathically said we had just mated for life. She felt me all over kissing and rubbing me, and stimulating me again and said to take her anyway I wanted. I had her kneel and put her head down as I got behind her and entered her, and did my earth doggie thing and fingered her ass, which drove her crazy and she screamed again and I could feel her vagina having spasms of pleasure. I pulled out and entered her ass, as I felt around and played with her swollen clit and pumped her as she screamed and then I came, and she collapsed on her stomach. I went to the bathroom and washed myself and my hands before returning and as she laid there I rubbed her back side. She slowly turned over reached up and pulled me to her and held me as she wrapped herself around me. I couldn't get loose, she was strong as hell. She must have realized that she was hurting me as she released me and apologized if she had hurt me. Lumia said the sex was so intense for her, and the pleasure was overwhelming. She promised no harm would come to me. I had planted the seeds necessary for her survival.

It was late evening after having returned home for about a week and I had went back to work and left Lumia at home with her device, as she watched television, watching all the different stations. I came home and she had figured out how the earth appliances worked and had fixed dinner. We ate and afterwards I told her it was time to rest after eating and sat up for a while before we went and bathed and then pulled the covers back on the bed and climbed in. I fell asleep and my body needed rest after returning to work and these new sexual exploits. Lumia wrapped her body around me and held me, I felt her next to me as I sleep.

When I woke it was nine hours later. Lumia was still in bed also. She woke when I did and read my thoughts. I needed to create and identity for her. I went and checked records and looked for a deceased person who would fit Lumia's description and acquired a copy of their birth certificate and social security card. Made copies then we went to the county and got a marriage license and then a new social security card, and a driver's license and then no one but us would know Lumia was and extraterrestrial. When we married she took it really seriously, and so did I. She explained when two people copulated on her world; it was part of the marriage ceremony and meant that they had become one for life. When we first had sex she had been willing not to abide by the custom, because she needed me to help her fulfill the chemical changes her body required. But now that we were married, according to her customs and those of earth, I was her husband and there was no way out. I could have female friends, but sex with them was forbidden, and she meant that.

Several months later, Lumia was pregnant, we went to the doctor and she said the embryos were healthy; Lumia was going to have triplets. As with earth females her stomach was large as well as her breast, but it wasn't nine months, it was eight. All were healthy, two boys and a girl. Lumia had talked to them while they were in the womb and when they were born, communicated with her and me. They grew and matured faster than human children and were very strong and healthy, talked all the time and were very smart, were walking at nine months and talking out loud at ten. I was amazed at Lumia body, she breast feed all three, and after a year they were fully weaned. Lumia body became more beautiful after giving birth, the expansion of child birth had completely reversed, and she was more feminine than before, her hips and breast were slightly larger, and waist was the same as before giving birth, she was lean and her skin was smooth and tight, not flabby. The children were exceptional reading before they entered kindergarten, and they soon advanced to regular school. They by earth standards they would be considered genius. Fun for them was reading the dictionary and studying other languages, by the time they were six years, between them each spoke seven languages, had mastered algebra, geometry and were reading at college levels. By ten they were at college levels, and we had to send them to a lab school at a nearby university because of their high intelligence. One majored in law and business, one in medicine, and the other in chemistry. Then they switched subjects between them. We adored them, and when we sat and ate as a family, I was so proud; they looked like both of us.

They were enrolled in a university at the age of thirteen, they finished multiple courses and having degrees in multiple subjects, and each one had mastered chemistry, medicine, math, physics, electrical engineering, and law. Each spoke twelve languages, and could read sign language. By the age of fifteen they had graduated from college. They asked me for one thousand dollars and started their own company, a consulting firm which made a half million dollars the first year. One started an electronics company, the other developed several new chemical applications, and the third, and our daughter was working as an archeologist. They took care of us, and knew about their mother and me and how different they were. We soon moved and had a new home built and the children had more space. It wasn't easy living with such intelligent children but they would explain to me anything I didn't understand. Our daughter told us a lot of the artifacts had been misinterpreted and she was writing a book that would straighten things out, and understood that the human race had been founded by extraterrestrials.

Lumia and I lived happily ever after and loved each other and sat in the evenings and looked at the stars and remembered that fateful night when we met on the wide open plains of Montana.

The End!

CHEATING WIFE

ISBN: 978-0-578-56641-2

Husbands Revenge

Cheating Wife

It all began a long time ago. Kavon Howard and Delia Howard were husband and wife. Delia was eight years older than Kavon. You wouldn't know it by her appearance, five, four and a half feet tall, cute, smooth brown skin, very short curly hair. Kavon was six, two in height, light skin with long curly hair. They meet at a local art fair. Delia had won second place at the fair, she was a perfectionist with her art, which was portraits done with pastel chalk on velour paper. She took commissions and would take a photograph from a client and enlarge it into a work of art. She had quit a job at a local bank to pursue a career in art and try to make a name for herself in the world of art doing portraits. Other than winning the art contest, she was only offered a spot in a local downtown restaurant doing quick portraits. It wasn't what she wanted to do with her art. She did meet her new husband though at the art fair. She walked around the fair that sunny June Sunday, when she spotted a rainbow of colors. She approached a small display of very large and colorful canvases, bright rainbows and landscapes, abstracts in a variety of colors. She approached a man standing with the display, she spoke to him and found out he wasn't the artist, but his friend who had come with him. She asked where he might be when Ken, Kavon's friend told her he was walking around the fair. She told Ken how beautiful the painting were and asked him to tell his friend about her display when he returned; she had to return back to hers. She returned to her display and several minutes later Kavon returned to his display. Ken told Kavon about the young woman who had inquired about his work and said she was cute and he should check her out. Kavon set out in the direction of Delia's display, it wasn't hard to find, and she was sitting and doing some quick portraits to make a few quick dollars. Kavon complimented her on her work, when she finished doing a quick portrait Kavon introduced himself to Delia.

She was delighted to meet him; he appeared as one of the best looking men she had ever seen. He took his time to talk to her and she was really interested in him also, they made a date for that evening after the fair, she wanted to celebrate her win and was a single mother with two nearly grown teens. Kavon said he would come over to her house, and bring a bottle of wine and they would celebrate together. She agreed that they would meet later and get to know one another. It was getting late and the fair was over at six pm. Kavon and Ken gather up his art work up and headed to his car. They headed back to Kavon's studio apartment on the eighteenth floor of a high rise on the lake front, on Chicago's south side. Kavon told Ken about his up and coming date, and was going to check out Delia. Ken said he had to leave because he had a hot date also, and said they would talk again soon. Kavon replaced his art back in the stack he had, based on picture size. Soon he was getting himself together for his evening with Delia.

Kavon had been married about five years before his wife asked him to leave. His ex-wife came home one evening after work, asked her eleven year old daughter to move upstairs with her grandmother, turned and asked him to leave. Kavon said, give him thirty days, it really took less, he had his job and it was all that really mattered to him. He had a feeling several days before that the marriage was about to end and had taken out a disclaimer ad in the local newspaper. You could do anything you wanted as long as you had a job. That's how he ended up in a studio apartment. Kavon didn't mind, hell he had a few girls who he treated to dinner and in turn, kept him sexually satisfied. He was happy with his apartment, had a great view of the south side facing west and bought some curtains that kept the heat out from the large windows which ran the width of the unit. It's where he saw some of those jaws dropping sunsets he painted. He loved colors, and used them in his work.

Kavon showered and dressed and prepared to leave, he would pick up a bottle of wine on his way. Delia was cute and he didn't care for large women and she seemed to be his type. There was a lot he didn't know now, but as time passed, he would slowly find out over time. Kavon rolled a few joints, was a weed smoker ever since his stint in the army. Had crossed both oceans, and saw enough of the world to know, there was no place like home. Took about seven joints of some really good weed, and headed out. Kavon drove to Hyde Park to his favorite liquor store, and purchased a nice red wine, it cost him about eight dollars, and a bottle of Champaign about the same price. He took his time driving, it being a weekend and warm with so many people out enjoying the summer weather.

When Kavon arrived at Delia's home, it was about eight in the evening, parked in front of her home. When he pulled up in front, saw it was a typical bungalow you would find all around the city, and had a side entrance. He exited his car and walked toward the side and the front entrance, pushed the door bell and waited for Delia to open the door. While he waited, noticed the neighbors' next door curiosity about his visit. Delia came and opened the door, and welcomed him inside. After entering he looked around and handed Delia the bottles to chill. Delia showed him around the house and he noticed it could use some work before they went and sat on some bean bag chairs she had and began to talk. She was the divorced mother of two older teens, her son twenty, who lived in the attic, and a daughter nineteen, an up and coming musician. Kavon told her he had a full time job as a repairman for the transit authority, and had been on the job eight years and was also divorced. He liked painting, and spent his spare time painting. His wages were enough for him to do his art, drive a car and eat, though he didn't go to clubs very often and found them a waste of time. Kavon liked getting high smoking weed and painting. Delia smoked weed also as Kavon handed her a joint, they smoked and found each other interesting and sexy. Delia brought a couple of glasses and the Champaign; they enjoyed the weed and Champaign and soon were sitting next to one another and started touching. Well one thing led to another and was soon they were in Delia's bedroom away from the prying eyes of her neighbors next door after sitting by a window. They had sex and enjoyed each other and were satisfied with their meeting. Kavon and Delia exchanged phone numbers, and really liked each other; of course sex helped a lot. Afterwards they smoked more and finished the Champaign before Kavon said he had to go because he had to work the next day, but promised to call the following day. He actually worked closer to her home than to where he lived.

Kavon departed and Delia didn't want him to leave, and decided to go home with him. She fell in love with him. Kavon didn't know what the future had in store for him. Slowly over several weeks he dropped his other female friends for Delia, and three months later they were married. He moved into her house along with her son, her dog and cat. Her daughter left seeking her fortune as a blues artist, and when her son made his twenty first birthday told her he wasn't taking care of another grown man, and he would leave if he didn't, the son left. The dog was old and had to be put to sleep and it was only the two of them and the cat. Kavon slowly made the needed repairs to the house and soon started making improvements. Every year they had a project to upgrade or repair the house. Finally she had met the man of her dreams, and was happy, but she was jealous and it showed. Kavon wasn't, and was always time after time being accused of having a woman on the side. Delia was happy and satisfied and when Kavon wanted her to dress in a tight dress and stockings and wig, before sex as fore play, she complied some times. It excited him and they had an active sex life. They shared a space for their art on the back porch and made it their studio; she was at one end, and him at the other. They were happy, or so it seemed.

Kavon had made himself a work shop in the basement after a while; putting glass block windows in the basement, steel doors and storm doors, and eventually their home started to stand out in the neighborhood by making the small improvements every year. Kavon and

Delia moved out for two years because she wanted a home that they had chosen together. She had a problem mentally with the home, was tired of the neighbors. After renting to friends for a year, and that turned out badly, because they were people Delia had bought her weed from. After them were her nieces, and they weren't the best tenants. Kavon wanted to move back, but first would rehab the house. There was three months before their lease was up at the apartment complex they had moved to. Kavon went in and tore out walls, and the bath and kitchen, it took him four and a half months, but he did it and Delia was overjoyed with the improvements. He added a half bath to the basement and made the home more functional. Soon they settled back down to a normal routine. Now remember the whole time Delia didn't work, other than keeping house and doing and occasional portrait. When Kavon couldn't smoke weed because of changes on his job, he drank a little more. Delia's girlfriend introduced her to a guy that did hair and Kavon had no problems with whatever she did, he wasn't the jealous one.

Kavon was totally ignorant of Delia's new adventures. When her sister came into a lump sum of money from a discrimination suit on her job, her sister bought an ounce of cocaine. Everyone partook and enjoyed it. Kavon snorted some and asked, where's the high, unlike smoking weed. It didn't do anything for him, until it made him horney, but for Delia it was another story. Delia sometimes seemed a little on edge; if he was five minutes later than usual, coming home from work she would accuse him of having a woman on the side. It never fazed him what was really going on. Kavon liked and enjoyed porno and had an extensive variety of vhs tapes, he also liked bondage and discipline and some sadism and masochistic videos. He had quite a few in his collection. He even painted some bondage scenes. Delia even bought some rope for him to use on her. Sometimes he would come home and she was happy, and on other days very uptight. She wasn't the easiest person to get along with, but he loved her. Then there was the money she couldn't account for, he had let her run the budget for the household and soon he couldn't get a straight answer from her. Kavon goofed around in his work shop and had bought a security system from a friend who had gotten a deal from some relatives who had broken into an electronics store. The system was the latest state of the art surveillance system, and decided to install it inside the house, and didn't tell Delia about it. Kavon was the radio and electronic sign man on the job and knew about electronics, had worked on radios in the military and since they had cable had wired the entire house when he did his rehab running cable to every room and internet and also had Wi-Fi. He had hidden the cameras when she was away getting her hair done or down the street at her girlfriend's house. He took over the money management when the bank contacted him about two small loans based on home equity and when they wanted their money. Delia didn't like it but couldn't answer where the money went, and Kavon was more concerned with his credit than anything. Things seemed to go smoothly afterwards, or so it seemed. He had the cameras installed and had all of the cameras up and running.

One day he returned from work and was surprised Delia was dressed in the sexy outfit he liked and was caught off guard by her wearing it. When he entered the back door and she greeted him and kissed and hugged him. Said she wanted him now, led him to the bedroom and was all over him. Usually he would take a shower because he smelled like diesel smoke from being around busses all day. He wanted to perform oral sex but she said no, and when he slid inside her she was wet, wetter than ever before. He didn't think anything of it then went and took a shower before returning then they sat and ate dinner. This was something new; she had never surprised him like this before, and didn't mind, he liked change, and she was happy. They had a normal evening and eventually went to sleep.

The next day she was going to have her hair done, and took the car, he had a van also, and drove it most of the time, the car was a lease. He went downstairs and opened his cabinet that he kept locked and decided to see what the cameras had recorded. The hard drive would hold several days, worth of video. Kavon looked at the videos, all the cameras were up and running, there were ten and he had covered the entire house, every room. He had a camera in the bedroom, dining, living, kitchen, both bathrooms, basement where the bar was there were two and the last one was on the back porch where they had there studio. He deleted the night time portions, and the normal everyday stuff giving more room on the hard drive. After fast forwarding for a short time, came across some very interesting stuff. That day she had worn her sexy outfit, well it turns out he wasn't the only one to have had sex with his wife. The reason her pussy was so loose and wet was he had sloppy seconds. Yes Delia was giving it up, and he saw why. She had a cocaine habit and that's why she couldn't or wouldn't explain where the money went. He watched as someone he didn't know came to the front door and she let him in, they went to the studio and she sat down, the cameras had audio and he could hear the entire conversation. The dealer or whoever he was had brought her a pretty good amount of powder. She had her mirror as he placed some on the glass and they cut it up with a card, made some lines and she sampled it. He snorted some also; she wanted the whole package but only had some of the money, she had $100.00 but he needed $140.00. He told her she could make it up in other ways. He said to her that some sex could make up the difference if she wanted to go along. She snorted another line, and said yes. Whoever he was, he wasn't bad looking, and she agreed to his terms. She smoked a joint he gave her and they got stoned together. She led him to the bed room and they undressed and she performed oral sex on him, he was well endowed, and she did for him, what she wouldn't do for Kavon. He watched as she worked her mouth over his very large penis, before he had her bend over doggie style and slammed it up her hot vagina, he was large and she moaned as he worked it in and out of her, smacking her ass with his hand, and telling her how nice her pussy was as she had her first orgasm and fell forward, as he turned her over on her back and entered her again, he pinched her nipples as she screamed and panted and he rammed her pussy and filled her with his come. Both were sexually driven by the cocaine they had snorted. They both dressed and went back and had a glass of wine before he departed. She went and wiped her dripping pussy but didn't douche. It was near time for him to return from work when she went and put on her sexy outfit. He saw himself come home and her having sex with him. Kavon now understood why she was so loose and wet; he had just had sex after she had fucked her pusher man.

Kavon wondered how long this had been going on before he had installed the hidden the cameras. He continued to go through the videos, and soon found another interesting scene. Her girlfriend Carla, which there was two, with the same name, only this was the cute very dark one from across the street, she came over and had some coke with her. They sat and had the mirror out and had some powder and made several lines, and had there straws and snorted several lines each and smoked a joint. Soon they were kissing and feeling one another before they headed to the bed room where they undressed. Carla only had a dress on, no panties and Delia had just a dress and panties. They ate each other out and both made the other climax as they returned naked to smoke more weed. They kissed as they felt each other and returned to the bedroom where Delia removed a double headed dildo and they fucked each other. They had both climaxed and soon dressed and returned and drank some more wine and finished smoking there weed. Carla returned home and almost two hours later before Kavon saw himself enter his home. That was all Kavon saw that had occurred within the past week, one encounter with the dope man and two with Carla. After deleting the unnecessary footage he burned to a disk all he found of these encounters and had no idea what else was taking place. The drive was clear and he filed away the disk he had just made. It would come in handy one day in the future.

Kavon fixed himself a drink and smoked a cigarette as he thought about all he had seen. Decided to go to the garage and get out the lawn mower so he wouldn't have this shocked looked on his face when Delia returned from her hair appointment. He cut the grass and cleaned out his van and was washing it when she returned home. She kissed him and asked him how her hair looked. It was very short and wondered why she was going once a month to get it done, since it was so very short. He told her it looked great and continued to wash his van. She returned inside the house after telling him she was going to fix dinner. Kavon and Delia had been married nine years now when he found out she was a cocaine user and was bi-sexual. Wondered how long before he let it out the bag. He was happy and could always use the videos in a divorce, but it would be better to use it against her and get her to do some of the perverted things that had running through his mind. He would use the rope she bought on her and not be overly excited so he could really have his way with her. Kavon had seen some really hot bondage and even some cruel ones also. Delia hadn't performed oral sex on him like she had on the pusher man and decided to see how much more would transpire before he made his perverted demands on her.

Several months passed and Delia seemed to become more comfortable with her promiscuous activities at home. Kavon observed one day as Delia was once again down the street with her girlfriend as he was going through the recordings of the past week, the dope man was back, and this time he had brought a friend. He had a nice quantity of cocaine. Delia was over joyed with it as she did a couple lines and was satisfied with the quality but was short on money as usual, and the man knew it. He and his friend did a couple lines and, told Delia, she could make up the difference the usual way. She agreed to the arrangement and they went into the bedroom, after undressing and going down on him the second man entered and disrobed. Delia started to protest, but the dope man told her, she wasn't nothing but a undercover hoe, and to keep sucking, the second man got behind her and fucked her from behind while her mouth was wrapped around the first man's very large penis, then they turned her around and she sucked the second man's penis as he came in her mouth and made her swallow his come. The first man proceeded to fuck her long and hard and soon she climaxed. She became the whore she really was then as she took his dripping cock in her mouth and then the second mans. They bent her over and fucked her sloppy wet pussy before fucking her in her ass, she screamed as they took turns with her and after a while they gave her some more coke. Soon she was on her knees with both cocks in her mouth. After filling her face with come they made her lick there asses which she willingly did without protest. They laughed and told her whenever she needed some powder to just call.

Delia turned out to be a real slut, constantly accusing Kavon of playing around on her, which he didn't. Kavon had several video discs of Delia and her cocaine escapades. He noticed her behavior more, wanted more money from him, but it wasn't happening. Kavon decided to treat his wife, he knew a guy on his job that had a good connection for cocaine, got him to get him an eighth of an ounce. He had enough of Delia's activities and would confront her over the next week end. That Friday after coming home and taking a shower, eating dinner and then sitting on the porch in there studio and having a drink, decided to surprise Delia. Told her he wanted her to dress like a whore, with the crotch less panty hose and the tube dress, high heels and nothing else and he would have a surprise for her. She went and changed with the hi-heel on and came over and he grabbed her and kissed the side of her face and felt between her legs. She wasn't wet yet and had bathed and douched before he came home. He had her mirror on the table and said he had a treat for them and dumped some of the cocaine out and began mixing it and made several lines and she snorted some and said she loved him, he snorted some to. He hadn't put all he had out, she was ready now, and he went and retrieved the collar and leash and some of the rope she had purchased for their sexual games. Came back as Delia was doing some more lines of coke, he came over and she was really in the mood now as he reached between her sexy thighs and felt her getting wet.

Kavon took and placed the collar around her neck, and attached the leash, whispered in her ear that she had been bad and needed to be punished for being such a slut. He had her stand as he tied her hands in back of her and led her through the house and to the bed room. He untied her hands and had her sit on the bed and pulled her dress up as he spread her legs and felt her. Told her she needed a shave, and was going to shave her pussy, she agreed to it and Kavon brought a razor and shaving cream and a bowl of water, he proceeded to lather Delia's vaginal area up and shaved her clean. Wiped her and then took the shaving equipment back before he returned with some oil and applied it to her freshly shaved pussy. Kavon told her to kneel as he tied her hands again behind her back and told her to suck his dick, she acted reluctant as he pulled on the leash, and said suck my dick whore, she resisted and he slapped her lightly, she was appalled. He said suck it like you suck your dope man's dick, bitch. She looked at him with a frightened look in her face as she opened her mouth and he cruelly rammed it in, holding her head on it until she started to gag. Kavon was determined to have his way with his bitch wife. He beat her face with his dick, while he told her he knew she was a slut and she was going to do whatever he wanted. He pulled the dress down exposing her very nice tits and played with her nipples as they became aroused before he reached over into a small bag and pulled out two clothes pins and attaching one to each nipple, she squirmed. He then made her stand, as he looked into her eyes and told her all about her exploits, fucking the dope man and his friend, and having sex with her girlfriend. At first she tried to deny what Kavon was saying, and then he told her she had two choices. He would leave her to her slut ways, or she would serve him as his sex slave and do whatever he wanted, whenever he wanted. That she had lied to him too often and he had enough and even fucked up the money from the bank. Delia begged for him not to leave her and would do whatever he wanted. Kavon pulled her dress up and walked her around the house, then made her stand at the back door, it was open and there was only the storm door that was closed. She begged him for forgiveness, and he told her he wasn't through with her. He untied her hands and told her to strip; she removed the dress and shoes, along with the stockings.

He led her downstairs to the basement where he placed cuffs on her wrist and attached ropes and then looped them through hooks he had installed in the high ceiling joist beams. She had her arms stretched out; Kavon then attached cuffs to her ankles, and then attached a piece of hand railing about two foot long with loops screwed in the ends to her ankle cuffs. He stood before her, and said I know everything, and it hurt him very much that she was a slut whore. She was facing the television on the bar as he turned it on and placed a disc into the player. Delia soon saw herself as Kavon sat and had a drink as she watched and cried, and begged him for mercy, while she watched Kavon placed a wide belt on the bar, along with some metal binder paper clips. He let it play all the way through; when he looked at Delia she was covered in sweat and had pissed on the floor. He walked over to her, told her how much he loved her but she had betrayed his trust, and he was going to let her feel how he felt inside. He rubbed her and she was really scared, but excited from the drugs. He felt her nipples and they were very sensitive, and then felt between her legs as the moisture began building, and he told her how she had given him sloppy seconds after fucking the dope man. She was going to feel the pain he felt inside as he picked up the belt, rolled it up and felt her all over with it.

He held her head with one hand and slapped her, said she was sorry as he slapped her again and then spit in her face. He gagged her before standing back and whipping her with the belt, she wanted to scream but couldn't now. Kavon replayed the video as he whipped her all over. He stopped and placed the metal clips on her nipples, and then he whipped her pussy repeatedly. When he stopped he felt her and played with her feeling her clit and pinching it until she climaxed. He pulled her dildo out and went behind her and reminded her how she had refused to have anal sex with him but had it with her dope man, as he spread her tightened cheeks and greased her up before inserting it up her ass, working it back and forth until she stopped resisting and gave in to the feeling, as he played with her clit and having a massive climax. Kavon removed the clamps from her swollen tits, playing with them as the feelings returned and they were even more sensitive. He took a piece of rope and tied around her waist and then between her legs holding the dildo in place in her ass, took the gag out, and took a strip of black cloth and after standing in her face and putting his fingers in her mouth, blindfolded her. He went and sat at the bar and just looked at her, sipped his drink, and thought what he was going to do next. To him she had presented him with the ultimate betrayal, and she had to pay for her sins and would the rest of her life with him.

After an hour Kavon decided he would lead her around like a dog before he fucked the shit out of her. He got up and went over and removed the blind fold. He kissed her and she tried to kiss him back as he stepped back. He untied the rope from around her waist and played with the dildo in her ass before pulling it out, untied her feet then her hands and had her kneel on hands and knees as he led her around like a dog, he sat at the bar and placed his shoes on her, he knew she had a thing about having feet on her and made her lay on her back and rubbed his shoes on her body and made her lick them. Told her kneel as he placed his hard dick in her mouth, she sucked his dick like never before. He stopped her and made her crawl over to a table where he had her stand and bend over, he fucked her pussy and she soon climaxed, he pulled out and entered her ass as he reached around and played with her clit, as she climaxed over and over again, and just when he thought he was going to climax had her kneel and suck him off, making her swallow all his cum. He pulled her to a standing position and said she was his slut, and she was going to do whatever he said, whenever he wanted it. Asked her if she understood, she replied yes. He said it's yes master, now bitch do you understand, and she replied yes sir master.

He ordered her to crawl to the steps leading upstairs before he told her to stand and go up. When they got upstairs, ordered her to shower, take an enema and a douche. When she had finished he ordered her to oil herself and put the dress back on with the shoes, he then placed the leather dog collar on her neck. He ordered her to stand before him with her arms folded behind her and her legs spread apart. Delia had the look of fear in her eyes as he looked at her, and reached between her legs and checked to see if she had cleaned herself. Told her to sit on her stool as he brought the mirror back to the table and poured some more coke on the glass and made some lines. He asked Delia if she wanted some, she said in a meek voice yes master. Delia was turned on and asked Kavon to kiss her. He told her to address him as master from this day forth. She said yes sir master, and asked him to kiss her, he said she could and she came over and kissed him and begged for his forgiveness. He told her, he would think about it. Kavon said he was hungry and wanted some Chinese food. Told Delia to get the menu and he would call in and order and they would go get it. She promptly did as she was instructed. He asked her what she wanted and he placed the order. Told her she was going with him and to make her face presentable, but she was wearing what she had on and nothing else. They soon left to pick up there order and Kavon ordered her out of the car and to come with him inside the restaurant. It wasn't ready yet and they had to wait so they had a seat, being out in public without any panties, and being treated like a whore was embarrassing to Delia and very exciting at the same time, their number was soon called and Kavon went to the window to get it and looked around at Delia sitting there looking coy and embarrassed, it excited him, after paying and taking there order he looked as Delia stood and her dress rose up, as she tried to pull it down, which excited him even more. They walked to the car and had her walk in front of him. After arriving home and backing in the garage and getting out, he had Delia bend over the table they sat at when outside in the garage, he pulled the dress up, spreading her thighs and she was soaking wet. He took his hard dick out and fucked her bent over the table until she climaxed. Then they headed inside the house to eat.

Delia attempted several times to return to her position of bossing Kavon around, and every time found herself strung up, whipped and fucked over and over again. Kavon didn't care about her fucking the dope man anymore, she tried to stop using coke, and only a few more times had the dope man over. Kavon told her he would know if she said anything about the cameras, and would be really sorry if she ever did. She paid for the coke as often as she could. But when she didn't have all the money, she gave up the ass. He even brought his friend over again, and they spent three hours using her, but she got her coke. They fucked her in her ass and pussy at the same time, made her lick there asses and just all around used her. They told her she was a slut, and that Kavon was stupid not to have her walking the street making some money. When Kavon saw that video, he used Dalia and made her crawl around the house and lick his ass; he pissed on her and spit on her. He was disgusted with her, and would teach her a lesson. He made her bath and oil herself, pushed and old lounge chair in the basement up against a vertical support beam, cuffed her hands above her head, then her legs. She was wide open for abuse, as he played with her pussy and while wearing a pair of latex gloves poured hot wax on her pussy and ass. Before using a blower to blow it off, the blower was powerful and her vaginal lips looked like a flag in the wind. He then used a vibrator on her. He played with her until she blacked out. He washed her while she was blacked out, and then brought her to. Delia was completely obedient and tried to stop using cocaine. Kavon made her get a blood test and checked for STDs, and fortunately she hadn't contacted anything.

After that Delia was the perfect wife, Kavon would take her out with little to nothing on and have her walk the street in front of him and then fuck her in his van. Every now and then she would try to reassert herself, only to find herself tied up, or humiliated at the hands of

Kavon. She kept the bathroom clean and especially the toilet, after Kavon had her crawling around and said she was thirsty and made her drink out of the toilet, she was totally submissive now to his whims. Every now and then he would treat her to some coke, and use her like a tramp. She dressed the way he wanted, and waited on him hand and foot. It was a happy relationship; it lasted nineteen years until Delia died in an auto accident. Kavon was heartbroken, but relived that her days of addiction were over.

Delia was laid to rest, Kavon moved on and found happiness.

The End

www.ingramcontent.com/pod-product-compliance
Lightning Source LLC
Chambersburg PA
CBHW070616120726
47909CB00004B/1237